Hurt Feelings . . .

"You mean, I'm not good enough to be a Unicorn?" Mandy demanded.

Jessica's eyes widened. "That's not what I said," she protested.

But Mandy paid no attention to her. "I may not have as much money as Lila Fowler or as many clothes as Janet Howell," she said through clenched teeth. "And I may not be as pretty as you are or as popular as Ellen Riteman. But that doesn't mean I'm not good enough to be a Unicorn!"

"I didn't say you weren't!" Jessica cried.

"That's what they're saying," Mandy retorted, "and you know it." Her eyes narrowed. "For weeks you guys have used me to run your errands, and now you tell me I'm not good enough for you? What snobs! I wouldn't be a Unicorn if you paid me a million dollars!"

Bantam Skylark Books in the SWEET VALLEY TWINS AND FRIENDS series.
Ask your bookseller for the books you have missed.

SWEET VALLEY TWINS
AND FRIENDS

Mandy Miller Fights Back

Written by
Jamie Suzanne

Created by
FRANCINE PASCAL

A BANTAM SKYLARK BOOK®
NEW YORK • TORONTO • LONDON • SYDNEY • AUCKLAND

RL 4, 008-012

MANDY MILLER FIGHTS BACK
A Bantam Skylark Book / May 1991

*Produced by Daniel Weiss Associates, Inc.
33 West 17th Street
New York, NY 10011*

Cover art by James Mathewuse

ISBN 0-553-15880-5

Published simultaneously in the United States and Canada

Mandy Miller Fights Back

One

◇

"Oh, no. Look at the time!" Elizabeth Wakefield glanced up at the clock in the hallway of Sweet Valley Middle School on Monday morning. "Only five minutes to the bell. Hurry up, Jess."

"But I can't find my book," Jessica groaned, frantically searching through her messy locker. She pulled out a pile of loose papers. "I don't understand. I'm sure I saw it just this morning."

"You did." Elizabeth couldn't help grinning at her twin. "It's probably still in your backpack. And your glasses," she added helpfully, "are in your pocket."

"Thanks," Jessica said. She pulled her book out of her backpack and fished in her pocket for her new glasses. Then she linked her arm in Elizabeth's. "I've got to admit, big sister, sometimes I don't know what I'd do without you."

Jessica and Elizabeth were identical twins, with the same long blond hair, blue-green eyes, and matching dimples in their left cheeks. But these days it was easier to tell them apart. Jessica was the twin with the glasses, which she was wearing temporarily. That wasn't the only difference between them. The two girls had opposite personalities.

Elizabeth was older than Jessica by four minutes, which often seemed more like four years. Her locker was always organized, while Jessica's looked as if a tornado had hit it. More important, Elizabeth tried never to be late to class. Jessica, however, always seemed to skid into the classroom at the very last second. The differences were even more noticeable when it came to the girls' tastes in hobbies and friends. Elizabeth enjoyed talking with her few special friends, reading books, and writing for *Sweet Valley Sixers*, the class newspaper she had helped to start. Jessica spent her time shopping for new clothes, gossiping about boys, and hanging out with her favorite Unicorns. The Unicorn Club was a group of the prettiest and most popular girls in Sweet Valley Middle School, and the members always tried to wear something purple, the color of royalty, to set themselves apart from everyone else. Jessica was proud to be a Unicorn, even though Elizabeth thought the group was rather stuck-up. She sometimes referred to them as "the Snob Squad" behind Jessica's back. Still, despite their differences, the twins were best friends.

Elizabeth smiled teasingly at her sister. "It's nice of you to admit that sometimes you can use a little help, Jess."

A girl came up behind them. "What kind of help do you need, Jessica?" she asked eagerly. "I'm available for homework, housework, baby-sitting, and running errands."

Jessica recognized the voice right away. It was Mandy Miller. She had been hanging around the Unicorns for weeks, offering to do anything for anybody. It had been obvious to the Unicorns that Mandy was trying to get into the club.

Jessica frowned. Mandy had been hanging around *her* more than any of the others. Every now and then Mandy would even hint that she wanted to be a Unicorn. Ordinarily, that kind of pushy behavior would have annoyed Jessica. But while Mandy was a nuisance, it was hard to be angry with her. She always wore a cheerful smile, and her clowning antics were very funny. Mandy's clothes were funny, too—weird combinations that looked as if they were homemade or came from the thrift store, often accented with dime-store or antique jewelry. Today, for instance,

Mandy was wearing jeans, an old purple sweat-shirt that said "Visit Chicago This Summer" in big yellow letters, and chunky yellow plastic bracelets on her wrists. Her splotchy purple sneakers looked as if they had been dipped in grape Kool-Aid. Her waist-length dark brown hair—she had the longest and prettiest hair Jessica had ever seen—was pulled back with a lacy yellow ribbon. Mandy wasn't beautiful, and her clothes were a bit strange. But Jessica had to admit that she had a certain flair.

Elizabeth glanced at the clock again. "Right now, Jessica needs help in getting to social studies on time," she told Mandy. "If she's late one more time, Mrs. Arnette is going to have a fit."

Mandy pushed up the sleeves of her sweat-shirt. "Well, let's get going, then. We don't want the Hairnet to blow a fuse." Mrs. Arnette was nicknamed the Hairnet because she always wore her hair in a net-covered bun at the nape of her neck. Mandy crossed her eyes and puffed out her cheeks. "Ff-ff-f-t!" she said, in imitation of Mrs. Arnette blowing a fuse.

Giggling, the three girls started down the hall. They hadn't gone far when Janet Howell came rushing up to them. Janet was an eighth grader, and president of the Unicorn Club. She smiled at Jessica, gave Mandy a distant and doubt-ful glance, and totally ignored Elizabeth.

"Jessica," Janet said, "we're having an important Unicorn meeting. Come on."

"Now?" Jessica asked. "But I've got to get to class. Mrs. Arnette will kill me if I'm late again."

"You can't miss this meeting," Janet warned. "It's crucial. And anyway, it won't take long. We'll be finished before the bell rings." She beckoned. "Come on. We're in the rest room."

Jessica shrugged helplessly and followed Janet into the rest room. Once she and Janet were inside, a Unicorn blocked the door so nobody else could enter.

"I suppose you all know why I've called this meeting," Janet said, looking around at the group importantly.

"I don't," Jessica spoke up. She sat down on a bench. "I hope it's going to be short, though. If I'm late to class again—"

"This meeting is about Mandy Miller," Janet interrupted. "This morning she asked me if she could join the Unicorns. I decided it's time we did something about her."

"We should have told Mandy off a long time ago," Lila Fowler said as she tossed her shoulder-length light brown hair. Lila was Janet's cousin, and the daughter of one of the wealthier men in Sweet Valley. "She's a nuisance. Whenever I turn around, there she is, doing her super-helpful routine." Lila sniffed. "She's so boring."

"She looks weird, too, in those strange clothes she wears," Ellen Riteman added. She perched on a sink. "They look like they came from a thrift shop. And today—" Ellen rolled her eyes. "*Today* she's wearing purple, of all colors. What makes her think she can wear *our* color?"

"We can't keep kids from wearing a color they want to wear," Jessica began, and then fell silent.

"I can't imagine why she thinks we'd ask her to be a Unicorn anyway," Kimberly Haver said haughtily.

Mary Wallace frowned from her seat on the windowsill. "It might be because we've encouraged her," she said slowly. "After all, we've asked her to do our errands. And we always laugh at her jokes."

"You're right, Mary," Jessica said. "We *have* encouraged her." Even though she agreed that Mandy wouldn't be a good Unicorn, Jessica was sorry to hear the way everybody was talking. "But just because Mandy's funny doesn't mean she ought to be a member of the club," she added quickly.

Lila nodded. "I agree with Jessica. Mandy's comedy routines can be amusing, but they're not suitable for a Unicorn. Mandy's not *cool*."

"Anyway, we can't afford to make another

mistake," Betsy Gordon warned. "Not after what happened with Brooke Dennis."

Jessica saw Lila blush. At Lila's suggestion, the Unicorns had invited Brooke to join the club, but she had turned them down. When word got around school, the Unicorns were extremely embarrassed.

Janet cleared her throat. "That's why Mandy has to be told she's got no chance of being a Unicorn," she said, and turned to look straight at Jessica. "And you're the one who's going to tell her."

"*Me?*" Jessica was surprised. "Why do *I* have to do it?"

"Because Mandy hangs around you more than the rest of us," Lila said firmly.

"Anyway, you don't have to be mean about it," Janet replied casually. "You can let her down easy. Just tell her we can't take any more members this year. Make up an excuse. We'll back you up."

Ellen nodded. "But whatever you tell her, tell her soon," she said. "I'm tired of her hanging around all the time."

"It really would be best to tell her now," Mary said gently. "It's not fair to give her false hopes."

"Exactly," Janet said. "Let's be fair."

Jessica frowned and pushed her glasses up on her nose. "I still don't see why I have to do it," she grumbled. "Anyway, Mandy's harmless enough. Why don't we just let her—"

"She may be harmless, but she's still a nuisance," Lila interrupted. "Besides, our reputation is at stake."

Jessica sighed. Mandy Miller just wasn't Unicorn material, that was all there was to it. And Mary was right, the sooner she was told the truth, the better.

At that moment the bell rang, and everybody scattered for class. Jessica was halfway there when she realized she had left her social-studies book in the rest room. By the time she finally retrieved the book, the late bell was ringing. Jessica dashed to the principal's office for a late pass, then raced to her class and slid breathlessly into her seat, five minutes late.

Mrs. Arnette had just finished dividing the class into pairs for a new project. "Jessica," she said sternly as she took the late pass, "I will not repeat the instructions you've missed. Your partner will tell you what to do. I will simply point out that this is the third time you have been late to class in the last month. Please stop at my desk before you leave class today."

"Yes, ma'am," Jessica said meekly, relieved that the Hairnet wasn't going to give her a lecture in front of her classmates. She looked around.

Who was this partner who was supposed to tell her what to do?

Then she heard a shrill whistle from the back of the room. "Jessica," Mandy called loudly. "Hey, Jessica, back here! I'm your partner!"

Jessica looked over her shoulder. Mandy was waving her arms. Several kids laughed at Mandy's antics.

Oh, no! Not Mandy Miller! Jessica groaned inwardly. She considered the possibility of telling Mrs. Arnette that she had to have a different partner. But when she looked across the room, she noticed that everyone else was already paired off.

"I'll bet you're wondering how we got to be partners," Mandy said happily when Jessica sat down beside her.

Jessica nodded slowly.

"Well, while you were at the Unicorn meeting—" Mandy began. Then she stopped. "That meeting," she said in a lower voice. "Was it about me?"

Jessica swallowed. How had Mandy guessed?

"After all," Mandy went on, "I heard Janet say the meeting was important, and from the look she gave me in the hallway, I thought maybe you were voting on me."

Jessica took a deep breath. Now was her chance to tell Mandy the truth and get it over with. But suddenly she felt very uncomfortable. It would be cruel just to blurt out the bad news. She shook her head. "No," she lied. "It wasn't about you. It was about . . . well, other Unicorn business."

Mandy nodded. "I understand," she said. She leaned forward. "But you *will* tell me as soon as they make a decision about me?"

"Sure, I'll tell you," Jessica said uneasily. She quickly changed the subject. "How did we get to be partners on this project, Mandy?"

"Well, it wasn't just luck," Mandy said playfully. "But this is your lucky day, Jessica. Everybody was begging to get me as a partner. They wanted my absolutely superior talent." Mandy grinned conspiratorially. "But I knew how crushed you would be if we weren't together. So I told the Hairnet you were the only person in class I would even remotely consider working with. That settled it. She had to give in and pair us up."

Jessica smiled weakly. She might have to work with Mandy, but she didn't have to like it. "What's the project?" she asked coolly.

Mandy dropped her playful tone. "It's really interesting, Jessica," she said. "You know we've been reading about the way things were in America in the 1920s."

Jessica nodded. She wasn't crazy about

schoolwork the way Elizabeth was, but social studies could be interesting.

"Our project has to have something to do with the way things were back then," Mandy went on. "For once, Mrs. Arnette isn't telling us exactly what to do. She wants us to use our imaginations and come up with a project that's unique and different. It's due on Friday."

"We're supposed to come up with something unique and different by *Friday*?" Jessica squawked. "But today's Monday! Most teachers give at least two weeks."

Mandy nodded. "Right. But this is different. See, a museum in Hollywood is putting on a big 1920s festival, and they've asked all the middle schools and high schools statewide to submit projects for a special exhibition. A jury will choose winners and award prizes. Mrs. Arnette just found out about it, and she thinks it would be a great honor if a project from our class won a prize in the exhibition."

"Maybe," Jessica said. "But if it's such a big deal, we should have more time."

"I agree," Mandy replied. "But the entries have to be in pretty soon. We have to have our school projects completed by this Friday so that she has time to decide which projects should be submitted to the museum festival next week."

"Well, I guess we'd better get started," Jessica

said. "Did Mrs. Arnette have any suggestions about what she thought was 'unique and different'?"

"Only the usual things. You know, book reports and stuff like that." Mandy shrugged. "Do you have any ideas?"

"Not right now," Jessica said. "Do you?"

Mandy shook her head no. "But we'd better think fast."

"OK," Jessica agreed, thinking, *the social-studies project isn't the only thing I have to think about.* She had to come up with a way to tell Mandy she was never going to be a Unicorn. Jessica sighed. To be fair, she would have to tell her soon. But it certainly wasn't going to be easy, particularly now that the two of them had to work together.

And as if she didn't have enough to worry about already, Mrs. Arnette had an unpleasant surprise for Jessica when she stopped at her desk on the way out of class.

Jessica went in search of Elizabeth at lunchtime. She found her twin at a table, talking to Todd Wilkins. Jessica didn't hesitate to barge in. What she had to ask her twin was far more crucial than anything Elizabeth and Todd could be talking about.

"Hi, Todd," Jessica said. "Elizabeth, I need to talk to you." She gave Todd a meaningful glance. "Alone."

Todd grinned. "I guess I can take a hint," he said as he stood up. "See you later, Elizabeth."

"Sure." Elizabeth grinned back at Todd. When he had gone she turned to Jessica and frowned. "What is it, Jess?"

Jessica sat down and took a piece of paper out of her backpack. "Did you get one of these midterm progress reports from Mrs. Arnette?"

Elizabeth leaned back in her chair. "No," she said softly.

Jessica tried not to look as anxious as she felt. "It looks bad. But what does it mean?"

Elizabeth sighed and opened her milk carton. "Mrs. Arnette talked about those reports before you got to class today, Jessica. She's decided to give progress reports to kids who aren't doing very well. The reports discuss what areas they have to work on."

Jessica glanced down at the report. It said "tardiness and inattention." And what was worse, there was a place for a parent's signature. She sighed. Her parents were not going to be happy about this.

"I don't see why all these things happen to *me*," Jessica said crossly as she stuffed the report into her backpack. "Getting a nasty note from the Hairnet is bad enough. I can't believe I have to work with Mandy Miller, too."

Elizabeth took a sip of milk. "Why don't you want to work with Mandy?"

"Because . . ." Jessica hesitated. If she told her twin what had happened at the meeting that morning, Elizabeth would probably say the Unicorns were acting like snobs. "Because she's such a . . . well, such a *clown*," Jessica said. "Those funny clothes, and that long hair hanging down her back—"

Elizabeth frowned. "Listen, Jess, you owe that 'clown' a lot. She got you out of a very tight spot."

"What are you talking about?" Jessica asked.

"I'm talking about what happened in class this morning," Elizabeth replied, "when Mrs. Arnette asked people to choose partners." She hesitated. "Nobody wanted to choose you."

Jessica stared at her sister. "What? You've got to be kidding. Lila and Ellen were there. *They'd* want to choose me." She lifted her chin. "I'm not exactly unpopular, you know."

Elizabeth looked at her twin sympathetically. "Lila and Ellen chose each other. The truth is, Jess, you've got a reputation for goofing around in class. Most kids don't want their grade to depend on you, no matter how popular you are."

Jessica scowled. "And just how do you know all this?"

Elizabeth put down her sandwich. "When

Mrs. Arnette called your name, somebody groaned. And somebody else said, 'No way.' After that, nobody would volunteer to be your partner. Mrs. Arnette wouldn't let me, since we're sisters. Mandy was the only one who was willing to take a risk with you, Jessica."

Jessica stood up. It had been nice of Mandy to choose her. And it was nice that she hadn't rubbed Jessica's nose in it. But that didn't change the facts. Working with her for a whole week was going to be terrible—not to mention that Jessica still had to figure out how to break the news.

Two

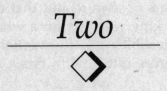

Lila and Kimberly met Jessica after lunch in front of Jessica's locker. "Well?" Lila asked. "How did Mandy take the news?"

Jessica shook her head. "I haven't told her yet," she said. "There wasn't time to say anything in social studies."

"I know," Lila said sympathetically. "I heard Mandy carrying on in class about being your partner. I really feel sorry for you, Jessica. It's not going to be easy working with her. Especially after you give her the news."

Kimberly sighed. "What a pain that girl is. I can't wait for her to stop hanging around us all the time."

"Don't worry about a thing," Jessica said confidently. "I'll tell her the next time I see her."

"Well, now's your chance," Kimberly hissed. "Here she comes—and look at those ridiculous purple sneakers!" With that comment, Lila and Kimberly hurried off.

Jessica turned to face Mandy. "Mandy," she said, "I've got something to tell—"

But Mandy interrupted excitedly, "Boy, am I glad I found you, Jessica. Listen, I've thought of a great idea for our project. You're going to love it!"

"What is it?" Jessica asked guiltily.

"Actually, my idea isn't easy to describe," Mandy said. "But I've got something at home that will show you what I'm talking about. Can you come home with me after school?"

Mandy was waiting excitedly for her answer, and Jessica couldn't think of an excuse for saying no. Anyway, she decided, it would be much better to tell Mandy about the Unicorns' decision in private, rather than at school. "OK," she said finally, "I'll go home with you."

"Great!" Mandy exclaimed. "This is going to be the greatest project ever, Jessica! The Hairnet will give us both an A when she sees it."

Jessica suddenly felt much better. If she got an A on the project, maybe Mrs. Arnette would forget about the bad midterm report. Working with Mandy might not be so terrible after all.

Mandy's house wasn't a typical suburban house like the Wakefields'. It was a big, rambling Victorian building in one of the older neighborhoods in Sweet Valley. Like Mandy, the gingerbread-trimmed house had a definite personality. Jessica's mouth hung open as they walked up the front path.

"Sort of grabs you, doesn't it?" Mandy laughed when she saw Jessica's face. "It's all that green and blue and purple woodwork."

Jessica nodded and tried to think of something complimentary to say. "It's pretty . . . unusual," she said at last.

Mandy shrugged. "Well, as my mom says, who wants to live in an ordinary house when you can live someplace really special?" She looked up at the house proudly. "My brother and sister and I helped my mom paint it."

"Didn't your dad help?" Jessica asked.

"He's dead," Mandy replied.

"Oh," Jessica said. She wished she hadn't been so tactless.

Mrs. Miller was in the dining room, sitting at a sewing machine. When she looked up from her work, her warm smile reminded Jessica of her own mother's. "I'm glad to meet you, Jessica," she said when Mandy had introduced them. "There are cookies and lemonade in the kitchen, girls. Help yourself."

"My mom isn't only the best seamstress in Sweet Valley," Mandy bragged, "she's also the best cookie maker." As they entered the kitchen, they bumped into a small boy with bright red hair, freckles, and glasses that had begun to slide off his nose. He held a pitcher of lemonade in one hand and a plate of cookies in the other.

"Well, look at this! It's the cookie monster," Mandy said, grabbing the boy's arm. "Hey, Archie, Mom didn't make that snack exclusively for you. You're supposed to share."

Archie hugged the pitcher and made a rude noise. "You're a pain," he said to Mandy.

Jessica laughed as Mandy poured some lemonade for Archie, gave him a handful of cookies, and sent him off. "I guess brothers are the same whether they're big ones or little ones," Jessica said. She was thinking of her fourteen-year-old brother, Steven, who raided the refrigerator at least three times a day and spent the rest of his time just being a nuisance.

"I guess," Mandy agreed as she arranged some cookies on a plate and poured two glasses of lemonade. "Sisters, too," she confided. "Now that my sister, Cecilia, is in high school, she thinks she can tell me how to behave. I call her

Saint Cecilia. Straight A's, never gets in trouble, does her laundry without Mom having to yell about it, that kind of thing." She grinned. "It's enough to give anybody a major inferiority complex."

Jessica laughed again. "Somehow I can't imagine you with an inferiority complex," she said.

Mandy wrinkled her nose. "Are you kidding? I'm always getting into trouble."

"I'm the same way," Jessica said. "Elizabeth has to bail me out of trouble all the time. It's almost like having an older sister." Jessica paused. She and Mandy actually had a lot in common.

The girls walked into a hallway. "That's our family photo gallery," Mandy said. She pointed to a wall covered with pictures, some of them old and faded. One showed a man wearing a striped suit and a white straw hat and carrying a fancy cane. Beside him stood a woman in a short white dress and a flapper-style haircut. "That's what I wanted to show you," Mandy said. She nodded toward the photo. "That's my grandfather and grandmother."

Jessica frowned. Had Mandy dragged her all the way over here just to show her a faded photo? "I don't understand what that old picture has to do with our project," she said.

"It's got everything to do with it," Mandy

replied excitedly. "My grandparents were in vaudeville. They came to California back in the 1920s to break into the movies. They never made it, and Granddad finally got a job selling insurance. But some of their old vaudeville costumes are still in a trunk in the basement."

"Their old costumes?" Jessica asked, suddenly interested. "You mean, their *stage* costumes?"

"Right!" Mandy exclaimed. "Now you've got the idea. For our project, we can do a vaudeville act, complete with authentic 1920s costumes! Mom can alter them for us. We can write the comedy routines ourselves, and we'll be the stars."

Jessica smiled. Mandy's idea was perfect. Mandy was a natural comedienne, and Jessica loved acting. With a good script and the right costumes, their project would be an enormous hit!

Mandy grinned mischievously. "Well, what do you think, Jessica? Isn't this the greatest project you ever heard of?"

"It's pretty terrific," Jessica agreed happily. "Where's the trunk?"

For the next fifteen minutes, the girls rummaged through the old trunk, pulling out dresses and jackets and scarves, the cane that Jessica had seen in the photograph, some silly fake wigs, and a droopy false moustache. They even found an old top hat and a moth-eaten white plush rabbit.

Mandy held up the rabbit by one ear. "I guess they thought a little magic would spice up their act."

Jessica grinned and picked up the fancy cane. Then Mandy stuck a straw hat on her own head. "Ladies and gentlemen," she announced loudly, "I am proud to introduce for your afternoon's entertainment the hottest new act in vaudeville: the one, the only, the original *Unicorn Sisters!*" She pulled off her hat and made a deep bow.

Jessica started to laugh, but stopped. "Hey," she said, "we can't call ourselves that."

"We can't?" Mandy asked. She frowned. "Yeah, I guess we can't. I'm not a Unicorn yet." Then she brightened. "But I might be by Friday. And anyway, I'll bet we can come up with some great Unicorny jokes." She poked Jessica with her elbow. "Get it?" she giggled. "Uni-*corny.*"

Jessica got it, but she didn't laugh. Now was the time to tell Mandy the Unicorns had turned her down. Mandy had given her the perfect opening. But somehow Jessica couldn't bring herself to say anything. *If I tell Mandy now*, she thought, *the rest of the afternoon will be spoiled.*

But for Jessica, the rest of the afternoon was already spoiled. While they worked on their project, Mandy laughed and giggled as usual. Jessica tried her best to laugh and look as if she were having a good time. But she just couldn't be enthusiastic about the project or at ease with Mandy. Jessica had a nagging feeling the Unicorns were making a mistake.

That night, Jessica was trying to decide what to wear to school the next day. She had narrowed down the choices to her green-and-white striped top and Elizabeth's blue blouse when her thoughts were interrupted by the phone ringing. "I'll get it," she yelled, and ran out to the hall.

It was Mandy. "Hi," she said. "Listen, Jessica, I was thinking that maybe we should stop at the school library tomorrow afternoon and check out some books on vaudeville. Maybe we could do a little write-up on the history of vaudeville to go along with our skit."

Jessica had to agree that writing a report was a good idea. But if the Unicorns saw her and Mandy together at the library, they were sure to harass her with questions later. And what if she ran into Aaron Dallas? Aaron was one of the cutest boys in sixth grade and Jessica's boyfriend. He was very nice, but Jessica was afraid he wouldn't like Mandy, particularly if Mandy was wearing one of her weird outfits.

"Jessica?" Mandy giggled nervously. "Are you still there? How about it?"

"Yes, I guess," Jessica said reluctantly. Suddenly an idea occurred to her that would make

Mandy a little less embarrassing to be seen with. Without thinking, Jessica said, "I've been thinking. You'd look really cute in my green striped top, Mandy. How would you like to borrow it tomorrow? You could borrow a skirt, too."

There was a silence on the other end of the line. Then Mandy said in a quiet voice, "No, thanks, Jessica. I think I'll wear my own clothes, if you don't mind."

Jessica bit her lip. "I didn't mean—"

"I know you didn't," Mandy interrupted. "But maybe this is a good time to level with you."

"Level with me?" Jessica asked uncomfortably.

"Yes," Mandy said. "Besides, once I'm a Unicorn, we'll be like sisters, won't we? And sisters don't hide things from each other."

Jessica cleared her throat. She *had* to tell Mandy about the Unicorns' decision. Maybe the best way to do it was over the phone. Then Jessica wouldn't have to see the look on Mandy's face when the news sank in. "Uh, Mandy," she began hesitantly, "there's something I'd better tell you—"

"Just let me finish," Mandy said. "The thing is, Jessica, I'm not the kind of person who likes to pretend to be something she isn't. I figured out a long time ago that I could never afford the kind of clothes you and the other Unicorns wear. In fact, I'd feel really stupid if I tried to fake everybody out by being a cheap imitation of a Unicorn. Then you'd never want me in your club."

Jessica winced. "Listen, Mandy, I—"

"So I decided I'd have my own style," Mandy went on. "It may be weird. But I don't want to look like everybody else anyway. I want to look like *me*. So thanks for your offer, but no thanks. Your green striped top is very pretty, but it isn't me." She paused. "Do you see what I'm saying?"

Jessica took a deep breath. Mandy was right. Her style was genuine, and Jessica had to respect that. "Yes, I do," she answered. "You have to be who you are. And if people don't like it, that's their problem."

"Right," Mandy said. "Now, if you wanted to trade me your denim jacket temporarily for one of my vests, that would be a different story. I really like your jacket. I could wear it with my black turtleneck."

"Terrific," Jessica said promptly. "How about letting me borrow the vest made out of old neckties?" Even though it was obviously homemade, Jessica thought it had a lot of style.

"Great," Mandy said. "I'll trade you anything I've got, Jessica. Except for my hair, that is." Mandy laughed. "It hasn't been cut since I was three, and I don't ever intend to cut it." She paused. "What was it you wanted to tell me a few minutes ago?"

"That?" Jessica swallowed. "Er, I . . . I don't remember," she stammered.

Mandy laughed. "That's OK. It'll come to you," she said. "Well, see you tomorrow."

"See you tomorrow," Jessica echoed, and put down the phone, a troubled expression on her face.

"What's the matter, Jess?" Elizabeth asked. She was standing in the doorway of her room, looking into the hall.

Suddenly, Jessica couldn't stand it any longer. She spilled out the whole story to Elizabeth. When she was finished, Elizabeth shook her head.

"I can understand why the Unicorns don't want her," Elizabeth said sarcastically. "After all, Mandy is a real person, and that makes them uncomfortable."

Ordinarily Jessica would have rushed to the Unicorns' defense. But right now she didn't feel like sticking up for them. Elizabeth might be right, but that didn't change anything. The fact was, snobs or not, the Unicorns had rejected Mandy, and it was Jessica's job to give Mandy the bad news.

Three

◇

At lunch on Tuesday, Jessica stood indecisively at the cash register in the cafeteria with her tray. Some of the Unicorns had already gathered at their regular table, the Unicorner. But Jessica didn't feel like eating with them today. She was looking around for Elizabeth when she heard a voice at her elbow.

"Move, Jessica, you're blocking traffic," Lila complained. Janet and Ellen were right behind her.

"Come on, Jessica," Ellen said. "Let's go sit down."

With a sigh, Jessica followed the girls to the table.

"Well, Jessica," Janet said as they sat down, "have you told Mandy yet?"

Jessica shook her head. "Not yet," she replied. "I only have one class with Mandy." She glanced at Lila. "Lila's in that class, too. She knows what went on this morning."

Lila gave a grudging nod. "The Hairnet was in a really bad mood."

Jessica was glad Lila had agreed with her. It was true that Mrs. Arnette had been in a terrible mood and that it had been impossible for anyone to talk. But what Jessica didn't admit to her friends was that she had met Mandy in the rest room early that morning to swap the denim jacket for the vest. The vest was in her locker right now. She didn't dare wear it at school because everybody would recognize it. But she was planning to wear it the first chance she got, when she'd be sure not to run into any of the Unicorns.

Though Lila had come to Jessica's rescue, she was not about to let Jessica off the hook. "I really think you should talk to Mandy," she said sharply. "You'll be seeing her soon to work on your social-studies project, won't you? Tell her then."

"Yes, Jessica," Ellen put in, "you've got to set her straight. This morning I overheard Bruce Patman telling Charlie Cashman that the Unicorns were taking in a weird new member. If we don't get rid of her soon, everybody will be laughing at us."

"I said I'd tell her, didn't I?" Jessica retorted. As a matter of fact, she had intended to give Mandy the news that morning in the rest room. But Caroline Pearce and Julie Porter had come in while they were trading clothes, and it had taken all of Jessica's wits to hide what they were doing. Besides, Jessica didn't want to risk Caroline overhearing her tell Mandy the Unicorns had turned her down. The news would have been all over school in a flash, and Mandy would have been completely humiliated.

"What I want to know," Kimberly Haver asked curiously, "is why Mandy is wearing your denim jacket, Jessica."

"My jacket?" Jessica asked in her most innocent voice, stalling for time. Her jacket was pretty ordinary. She hadn't thought anybody would recognize it as hers. "How can you be sure it was my jacket she was wearing?"

"I saw it, too, Jessica. It had to be yours," Mary Wallace said. "Remember when you put your elbow down on Aaron's candy bar? Your jacket still has chocolate on the sleeve."

Ellen frowned. "Maybe she stole it out of your locker, Jessica."

Jessica was momentarily speechless with fury. She couldn't believe that Ellen was accusing Mandy of stealing! But she couldn't let the Unicorns know the truth. She kept her voice calm. "I don't think Mandy would do anything like that," she said. "I'll bet Elizabeth loaned the jacket to her. I've told her over and over again not to loan my clothes without asking me."

"That's probably what happened," Mary agreed. She sounded relieved that Jessica had gotten Ellen off the subject of stealing. Jessica smiled at her. She had the feeling Mary liked Mandy, too.

"I didn't know Mandy was friendly with Elizabeth," Kimberly remarked.

"Mandy's friendly with everybody," Jessica said. She laughed nervously.

"*That's* the truth," Ellen commented. "And it's another reason why she's not Unicorn material. She's not at all selective about whom she socializes with."

"If you don't tell her today, Jessica," Lila warned, "I'm afraid either Ellen or I will have to break the news to her."

Jessica was growing more alarmed by the minute. She knew it would be even more painful for Mandy if Lila or Ellen relayed the message.

"Anyway, Jessica," Janet said kindly, "you have such a wonderful way with words that Mandy probably won't even care that we've turned her down."

"Thanks, Janet," Jessica said a little sadly. She knew that Janet was wrong. Mandy *was* going to care about being turned down. She was going to care a lot. More than anything else, Mandy wanted to be a Unicorn. And at this moment, Jessica couldn't imagine why.

After lunch, Jessica was getting a book from her locker when Elizabeth came hurrying up to her.

"I'm glad I found you, Jess," Elizabeth said breathlessly. "I want you to hear this." She pulled a piece of paper out of her notebook.

"What is it?" Jessica asked as she closed her locker.

"Caroline Pearce turned in her *Sixers* gossip column this morning. There's something about Mandy in it," Elizabeth replied. She began to read. " 'Word has it that the members of the most elite club at Sweet Valley Middle School have told hopeful Mandy Miller to buzz off and quit bugging them. But cheer up, Mandy. There are lots of people who *aren't* Unicorns.' "

"Oh, no," Jessica moaned.

"Oh, yes," Elizabeth said grimly. She crumpled the paper and tossed it into a nearby garbage can. "I told Caroline we couldn't print this. But she said everybody knew it anyway."

"That's awful, Elizabeth," Jessica said. She

shook her head dismally. "I guess I'd better tell her right away."

"You'd better," Elizabeth agreed soberly. "Unless you want her to hear it from somebody else."

After the last bell, Jessica and Mandy stopped at the school library and checked out a couple of books for background research. Then they walked to Mandy's house to work on their project. On the way, Mandy chattered happily while Jessica waited for a good opening. She wanted to let Mandy down in the kindest way possible.

Jessica's best chance came when they were going up the walk to Mandy's house. "By the way," Mandy said, "I bumped into Ellen Riteman this afternoon, and she said something funny. She asked if I'd talked to you lately. When I asked her what you and I were supposed to talk about, she just shrugged." She looked at Jessica curiously as she opened the front door. "What's going on?"

"Well, to tell you the truth—" Jessica began. She was interrupted by Mrs. Miller, who called out to them from the dining room.

"Hi, Mom," Mandy said. She glanced at what Mrs. Miller was sewing. "How are you doing with our costumes?"

"Just fine," Mrs. Miller replied, smiling. "They'll be finished tomorrow." She looked back at her sewing. "You'll find some chocolate-chip cookies and lemonade in the kitchen. Help yourselves."

"Great," Mandy replied. "Chocolate-chip is my favorite. Come on, Jessica."

The girls went into the kitchen, where they found Mandy's little brother, Archie, piling cookies on a plate. A large, evil-looking green lizard, its tongue flicking in and out, was perched on his shoulder.

"What . . . what's that?" Jessica asked.

Archie grinned wickedly. "Haven't you ever seen an iguana?" he asked. He pulled the lizard off his shoulder. "His name is Ignatius. Iggy for short."

Jessica backed away. "I don't think I—"

"What's the matter?" Archie asked, grinning even more wickedly. "You're not afraid of him, are you?" He thrust the lizard toward Jessica. "He's just a harmless little iguana. He only wants to crawl up your arm and hide under your hair."

Jessica yelped and darted to the far end of the kitchen table. "Mandy," she cried, "tell him to put that thing away!"

Mandy grabbed Archie's shoulders and swung him around. "Take your cookies and scat, brat," she said. "And take that stupid lizard with you."

"Aw, Mandy, I was just having some fun," Archie grumbled.

"Have fun somewhere else," Mandy ordered. She swatted him away. "Go!"

Jessica waited until Archie and Iggy were safely out of the kitchen before she came out from behind the table. "Thanks, Mandy," she said gratefully. "Lizards aren't my favorite animals."

Mandy picked up the pitcher to pour Jessica's lemonade. "Archie's lizards aren't so bad. It's his snakes that bother me. Sometimes one gets loose and shows up in a weird place, like the bathtub." She laughed. "I hope you never get a little brother, Jessica, or even a little sister. They can really make you crazy."

Jessica shuddered. Her older brother had his faults, but at least he didn't collect snakes and lizards.

Mandy handed her a glass. "Now what were we talking about?"

Jessica cleared her throat. "We were talking about—"

"Hi, you two." The girl who came into the kitchen was taller than Mandy and her hair was darker, but Jessica knew she had to be Mandy's sister, Cecilia.

"Hi, Ceci," Mandy said. "This is Jessica."

Cecilia smiled at Jessica. "I hope you left me some lemonade, Mandy."

"There's plenty," Mandy said. But just as she was about to hand the pitcher to Cecilia, it slipped from her fingers and fell with a crash to the floor. The pitcher smashed in a dozen pieces and lemonade splashed everywhere. Jessica jumped back.

"I can't believe I did that," Mandy said, staring at the mess.

"I can," Cecilia said. "Last night it was a full plate of spaghetti, remember? With sauce."

Mandy rubbed her right arm. "I remember. It just slipped out of my fingers."

Jessica looked at Mandy. "Did you hurt your arm?" she asked.

Mandy shook her head. "I don't think so." She went to a broom closet for a mop. "As soon as I've cleaned up this mess, we can get started on our project."

Cecilia took the mop away from her. "Go on and work on your project," she said. "I'll take care of this."

Mandy looked at her sister gratefully. "What did I tell you?" she said to Jessica. "She's Saint Cecilia."

Cecilia laughed. "That's OK. You can make it up to me by doing the dishes tonight."

Jessica had to giggle. Mandy and Cecilia were a lot like her and Elizabeth.

Carrying their snacks, the girls went upstairs to Mandy's room. "I wrote out a script for a couple of routines," Mandy said. "I want to know what you think of them."

Jessica knew Mandy had forgotten what they had been talking about earlier, and at the moment she couldn't think of a tactful way to bring it up. Instead, they read through Mandy's script. One of the pieces was an old favorite of Jessica's, the Abbott and Costello "Who's on first" gag. The girls went through the routine a few times, just for the fun of it.

"I made up the rest of the routines," Mandy said. "Some of them might be a little corny."

"That's OK," Jessica replied. "It wouldn't be vaudeville if it weren't a little corny!"

"See what you think about this one," Mandy said, turning a page of her script. "We're standing on a street corner, waiting for a bus. I act really surprised, and I say, 'Hey, Jessica, did you see what I just saw?' You say, 'No, Mandy, what did you see?' And I say, 'I just saw the weirdest thing. It was a *unicorn* walking down the street, wearing *two* pairs of purple sneakers.' And you say—"

"Stop!" Jessica cried. She put her hands over her ears.

"Is it too corny?" Mandy asked anxiously. "The original joke was about an elephant, but I thought that because you're already a Unicorn and I may be—"

"You're not going to be a Unicorn, Mandy," Jessica blurted out.

Mandy stared at her. "What?" she whispered.

Jessica could have bitten off her tongue. She had meant to lead up to it gently, and instead she had been absolutely tactless. "The Unicorns decided that you weren't . . ." she stammered. "I mean, we decided not to . . . I mean—"

Mandy's eyes were fastened on Jessica's. "When did you decide this?" she asked.

"Uh, in the rest room," Jessica said slowly. "Yesterday morning."

"You mean, you've known for two days and you didn't tell me?" Mandy cried.

"I tried," Jessica said desperately. "I really did. But every time I started, something happened and I couldn't—"

"Why?" Mandy demanded.

Jessica looked down. "I just told you," she said. "Every time I started to tell you, something—"

"Why did you turn me down?"

Jessica didn't answer right away. All she could think of right now was what snobs her friends were, and how wrong it was for them to have rejected Mandy. "I don't see why you want to be a Unicorn anyway," she said finally. "You're not anything like the others. Why would you even consider it?"

"You mean, I'm not good enough to be a Unicorn?" Mandy demanded.

Jessica's eyes widened. "That's not what I said," she protested.

But Mandy paid no attention to her. "I may not have as much money as Lila Fowler, or as many clothes as Janet Howell," she said through clenched teeth. "And I may not be as pretty as you are, or as popular as Ellen Riteman. But that doesn't mean I'm not good enough to be a Unicorn!"

"I didn't say you weren't!" Jessica cried.

"That's what *they're* saying," Mandy retorted, "and you know it." Her eyes narrowed. "For weeks you guys have used me to run your errands, and now you tell me I'm not good enough for you? What snobs! I wouldn't be a Unicorn if you paid me a million dollars!"

Jessica could feel herself getting angry. "Just a minute, Mandy," she snapped. "You're the one who started hanging around the Unicorns, offering to do things for us. *You're* the one who was using *us* to get yourself into the club."

"That's stupid!" Mandy shouted. "I've been hanging around because I wanted you guys to notice me. Most of the time you've got your noses so high in the air, you don't notice anybody but yourselves. And I clown around because that's the way I am. And I offer to help because I want to be nice to the people I like, such as you, Jessica."

Jessica could feel the anger rising in her throat, anger mixed with embarrassment. Everything Mandy was saying was true, but Jessica was a Unicorn, too. An insult to the club was an insult to her. "You used me," she muttered. "You picked me for a partner in social studies because you thought I'd put in a good word with the Unicorns."

"That's stupid, too!" Mandy scoffed. She folded her arms across her chest. "I picked you because nobody else would. I picked you because I'm your friend."

Jessica stood up. She knew her face was red. "Some friend," she muttered. "Making a big fuss just because the Unicorns turned you down."

Mandy snorted. "What do *you* know about being a friend, or about standing by somebody who needs you? All you and the Unicorns know is how to *use* people."

Jessica started for the door. "I've had enough," she said. "I'm leaving."

"Good," Mandy answered. "And don't come back." With that, she slammed the door after Jessica.

As she walked, Jessica found herself blinking back tears. When she got home, she rushed up the stairs, flung herself on her bed, and buried her head under her pillow.

Elizabeth found her a few minutes later. "What's the matter, Jess?" she asked, sounding concerned. "Are you sick?"

Jessica pulled the pillow off her head and rolled over. "I told Mandy," she said, rubbing her eyes with her fist.

Elizabeth handed her a tissue. "Was she upset?"

"She was *mad*," Jessica said. "I really blew it, Elizabeth. I meant to tell her she was too good to be a Unicorn. Instead I made it sound as if she weren't good enough."

Elizabeth sighed. "That's too bad, Jess. I'm sorry."

"I am, too," Jessica replied. She blew her nose. "I'm mad at myself for messing things up. And Mandy didn't make me feel any better by saying all that stuff about the Unicorns."

"What stuff?" Elizabeth asked gently.

Jessica wiped her eyes. "About what snobs the Unicorns are."

Elizabeth raised her eyebrows. "Well, what would *you* call them? At least as far as Mandy is concerned."

Jessica sighed. "Snobs, I guess. Me included." She shook her head. "Poor Mandy. I feel sorry for her. And I feel sorry for *me*, too. I've lost a friend.''

Elizabeth stood up. "It's not over yet,'' she said. "Mandy will cool off.''

"I doubt it,'' Jessica said glumly. "But at least Janet, Lila, and Ellen got what they wanted. Mandy won't be hanging around the Unicorns anymore. She said she wouldn't be a Unicorn for a million dollars.''

Four

◇

Lila and Ellen were waiting expectantly for Jessica
Wednesday morning in homeroom.

"Well?" Lila asked. "Did you do it?"

Jessica dropped her books on her desk with
a bang. "I told her."

"Terrific!" Ellen said, clapping her hands.

Lila leaned forward. "Tell us all the details,
Jessica. How did she take it?"

"Yes, tell us, Jessica," Ellen echoed. "What
excuse did you give her?"

For a second, Jessica hesitated. She wanted to
tell Lila and Ellen the truth—that she had messed
everything up, and that she felt miserable about
it. But nothing between Mandy and Jessica would
change if she told her friends what had happened.

Her friendship with Mandy was finished. "I just told her straight out," Jessica said at last. "She was upset, but I think she'll get over it."

Ellen's eyes widened. "You just told her like that?" she asked. "That means she couldn't make any mistake."

Lila nodded knowingly. "Yes, it's much better to tell the truth in a case like this than to beat around the bush." She smiled. "Janet will be so glad you've done such a good job, Jessica."

Just now, Jessica didn't really care what anyone thought. All she could think about was how rotten Mandy must be feeling. She felt pretty rotten herself.

As Jessica sat at her desk feeling miserable, Lila and Ellen began to talk excitedly about the project they were planning for social studies.

"I just know Mrs. Arnette will enter our project in the festival," Ellen said smugly. "It's so unique."

"Really?" Jessica asked, relieved that the subject had been changed. "What are you doing?"

"It's a secret," Lila said. "We're not going to tell anyone because we don't want anyone to steal our idea."

Jessica frowned. Was Lila suggesting *she* would steal their idea? That was ridiculous. The project she and Mandy were working on was so good, they didn't need to steal ideas from anybody.

Later that morning in social studies class, Mrs. Arnette announced that the students should sit with their partners, discuss their projects for a few minutes, and give a brief report to the class on what they were doing. Jessica was pleased. Now Lila and Ellen would have to expose their big secret.

Mandy walked over to Jessica's desk. "I'm returning your jacket," she said. She dropped a brown paper bag in front of Jessica. "I didn't want to wear it, under the circumstances."

"Your vest is in my locker," Jessica answered. She couldn't meet Mandy's eyes. "I'll get it for you later."

Mandy gave a short, bitter laugh. "I'll bet you never even dared to wear it." She sat down next to Jessica.

Jessica felt her cheeks get hot. "What are we going to tell the class about our project?" she asked, dodging Mandy's comment.

Mandy shrugged. "We could do one of the routines," she suggested. "Let's see. Maybe the one about the unicorn and the purple sneakers?"

Jessica frowned. "I don't think that would be a good idea," she said. She glanced uncomfortably over her shoulder at Lila and Ellen.

"Then let's do Abbott and Costello," Mandy suggested.

When it was their turn, Jessica and Mandy clowned their way through the famous old vaudeville routine. By the time they finished, Mrs. Arnette was wiping tears of laughter from her eyes.

"Bravo, Mandy! Bravo, Jessica!" she cried, clapping so hard her bun bounced on the back of her neck. She turned to Jessica and whispered, "If you do as well on Friday, Jessica, I shall have to reconsider the negative progress report I gave you earlier in the week."

Jessica and Mandy headed back to their seats. Elizabeth and Amy Sutton were on their way to the front of the class to give their report. "That was a terrific act, you guys," Amy said.

"It was really funny," Elizabeth agreed. "You two are a great team."

Mandy gestured in the direction of Lila and Ellen. Neither of them were smiling. "I don't think Jessica's *friends* liked it," Mandy remarked.

Jessica shrugged. Lila and Ellen were actually frowning. What was wrong with them? "Maybe they need a sense of humor," she remarked.

"Well, if that's their problem," Mandy replied, "there's nothing I can do for them."

The two girls sat down and Mandy leaned toward Jessica. "By the way, Jessica," Mandy whispered, "my mom finished our costumes. If you can come over after school, we could have a dress rehearsal."

Jessica glanced in Lila's direction. Lila's eyebrows were raised questioningly.

"On the other hand," Mandy said quickly, "if you've got something to do with the Unicorns, I'm sure we can get by without another rehearsal."

Jessica turned away from Lila. "I'll come," she said. Then she settled back to wait for Lila and Ellen to report to the class on their project. But to her disappointment, the bell rang before their turn. Jessica would have to wait until Friday to discover their big secret.

Jessica wasn't sure she should have accepted Mandy's invitation to go home with her that afternoon. Lila and Ellen had been upset when she had turned down their invitation to go to the Dairi Burger after school. It also occurred to Jessica that Mandy had probably told her whole family that the Unicorns were a bunch of snobs and that Jessica was the biggest snob of them all. And she didn't think being with Mandy was going to be much fun. It was obvious that Mandy was still holding a pretty major grudge.

But when Jessica and Mandy arrived at the Millers' house, Mrs. Miller was just as friendly as ever. She had laid out the costumes in the dining room and she helped the girls try them on, using pins to adjust a hem or a sleeve. Jessica's costume was a short red dress, flapper style, which she would wear with lots of shiny beads and bracelets. Mandy's costume was a white dress with red trim and her grandfather's white straw hat with a jaunty red band. Both girls carried walking sticks they had found in the trunk.

"You look great," Mrs. Miller said approvingly. "But I don't know what you're going to do with your hair. Long hair wasn't in style in the 1920s, you know."

Mandy frowned. "What we need are a couple of wigs."

"Weren't there some in that trunk?" Jessica asked.

"We'll look as soon as we've had something to eat," Mandy decided. "Let's see what we can find in the refrigerator."

In the kitchen the girls met Archie, with Iggy on his shoulder. Archie was making himself a huge peanut-butter-and-banana sandwich. He smiled at Jessica and reached for his iguana.

"No, you don't," Mandy said hurriedly. She handed him his sandwich and a glass of milk. "Now *go*." She turned to Jessica. "Can I make you a sandwich?" she asked.

"Peanut butter would be fine." Jessica sat down on a kitchen stool. She couldn't figure it out. Since they had left school that afternoon, Mandy had been acting as if nothing had happened. Did that mean she was ready to forgive and forget? Jessica was about to ask her when Cecilia joined them.

"Hi, Mandy. Hi, Jessica," Cecilia said cheerfully. "You're not going to spill any more lemonade, are you, Mandy?"

"Not if I can help it." Mandy grinned.

"I hope not," Cecilia said, "because I don't have time to mop today. I have to go to the store for Mom."

"Yes, Saint Cecilia," Mandy said, rolling her eyes.

"You know, Mandy," Cecilia said, "you could help Mom more than you do."

"I help enough," Mandy retorted.

"Just barely." Cecilia smiled at Jessica. "See you guys," she said as she left the kitchen.

Jessica watched her go. It was clear that if Mandy had told anyone in her family what had happened, they weren't blaming Jessica. But their attitude only made Jessica more uncomfortable. She couldn't apologize for the awful way the Unicorns had treated Mandy. But she could apologize for losing her temper and yelling at her friend.

Mandy handed her a sandwich. "Mandy," Jessica said, "I want to tell you that I—"

Mandy frowned. "If you're going to talk

about what happened yesterday, I think we should forget it.''

"Forget it?" Jessica asked. "But I really want to apologize for—"

"What I mean," Mandy said thoughtfully after taking a bite of her sandwich, "is that I've decided you're right, Jessica. I'm not like any of the Unicorns. I may be a little weird, but I'm me, and I intend to stay that way. And I don't care whether the Unicorns like it or not."

Jessica felt a great sense of relief. "You're not mad at me?"

"Well, I was," Mandy confessed, "when you said all that stuff about my using the Unicorns. But then, when I really thought about it, I decided you had a point. Maybe I did go out of my way to get you to pay attention to me." She grinned ruefully. "Sometimes I overdo things a bit."

Jessica nodded. "Maybe. But I think you were right, too. We, I mean the Unicorns, sort of got into the habit of using you, until . . . until . . ." Jessica stopped. If she kept talking, she was probably going to say something stupid again.

Mandy finished Jessica's sentence. "Until I got to be too much of a nuisance?" she asked. "Was that what you were going to say?" She grinned crookedly. "Don't worry, I'm not going to get mad again. You see, I know something the Unicorns don't."

"You do? What?" Jessica was curious.

"I know they made a mistake when they turned me down," Mandy replied confidently. "And I have an idea that sooner or later they'll realize it." Mandy smiled. "In the meantime, I don't think there's any point in us being mad at each other. Do you?"

Jessica shook her head emphatically.

"OK, good," Mandy said. "We'll forget it ever happened." She stuffed the last of her sandwich into her mouth. "Come on, let's look for those wigs." The girls headed for the basement.

The trunk stood open in a corner of the room. The girls rummaged through it and found a pair of black patent-leather tap shoes, an old baseball cap, and a big black purse. Finally, they pulled out a box that contained a slightly moth-eaten short red wig and an even shorter brown one. Jessica looked at them uncertainly.

"I don't know," she said. "They look kind of dumb."

Mandy grinned. "This is vaudeville, remember? We're not trying to win a beauty contest. The funnier the better."

Jessica laughed and pulled on the red wig with ease. It took more work to tuck all of Mandy's long hair up under her wig, but eventually they succeeded.

"Well?" Mandy asked. "How do I look?"

"Weird." Jessica laughed. "How about me?"

"You look weird, too," Mandy said. "We're a pair of weirdos."

Mandy turned back to the trunk and started digging deeper. "I wonder if there's anything else in here we can use?"

Suddenly Jessica spotted a fluffy pink feather boa. "I'd like to wear this," she said. She picked up one end of it.

But at that same moment Mandy picked up the other end. "Hey, this would look cute with my outfit," she exclaimed.

"I saw it first," Jessica retorted as she pulled on her end.

"But it's in *my* trunk," Mandy said, tugging on hers.

Each girl yanked one end in a silent tug-of-war. Then, without warning, the feather boa tore and Jessica landed against the basement wall with a thud. Mandy tumbled backward over the trunk, still clutching her half of the pink feather boa.

Jessica straightened up and rubbed the back of her head. She looked around. "Mandy?" she called.

For a moment there was silence. Then Jessica heard a loud sneeze. "Mandy?" she called again. "Are you all right?"

Mandy appeared from behind the trunk. She laughed and rubbed her right side by her ribs.

"Yeah, I'm all right," she said. She held up her half of the feather boa. "Here, you can have it if you want it."

"Thanks a lot," Jessica said dryly. "What good is half a boa?"

"Half a boa is better than none." Mandy giggled. "Give me a hand, will you?"

Jessica reached over the trunk and helped Mandy to her feet. "Are you sure you're OK?" she asked.

"I'm sure," Mandy replied, still rubbing her side. Then she felt under her right arm. "Hey, I got a lump—" She frowned. "But it was my ribs that I bumped, and that's not where the bump is."

"Maybe we could write the fall into our act," Jessica suggested.

Mandy nodded. "Maybe. Well, now that we've done our tumbling routine for the day, how about that dress rehearsal?"

"Sure," Jessica said. "Hey, Mandy, remember that joke about the unicorn with the purple sneakers?"

"The one that upset you yesterday?" Mandy asked.

Jessica grinned. "Yes, that one. Well, I'm not upset anymore. Let's do it."

Mandy arched her eyebrows. "You're not kidding?" she asked. "You really want us to joke about the Unicorns?"

"I'm not kidding," Jessica said. She thought of Lila's and Ellen's sour faces. All the other kids in Mrs. Arnette's class had loved the jokes. "What the Unicorns need is a sense of humor."

Mandy grinned. "Yeah, I'll go along with that," she said.

For the rest of the afternoon, Jessica and Mandy clowned their way through their routines, getting better and better each time they rehearsed a gag.

"If we're this good on Friday," Mandy said when they finally called it quits for the afternoon, "Mrs. Arnette will give us an A for the entire *term*."

Jessica laughed. "I could use all the A's I can get!"

After a few more hours of rehearsal on Thursday afternoon, Jessica and Mandy were ready to present their completed project to the class on Friday morning. Most of the students had taken the project seriously, and many had produced interesting work. Winston Egbert and Tom McKay had teamed up to build a model of the *Spirit of St. Louis*, the airplane Charles Lindbergh flew solo across the Atlantic in 1927. Elizabeth and Amy had videotaped silent films from the television and had

written a report on the beginnings of the Hollywood movie industry. Randy Mason and Pamela
Jacobson had assembled some pictures and written a report on the stock market crash of 1929.
The book report that Lila and Ellen had written
seemed pretty ordinary in comparison to the other
projects. Jessica couldn't figure out why they had
wanted to keep it a secret.

But Jessica and Mandy were the biggest hit in
the class. Everyone laughed at the routines, and
at the costumes, wigs, and other props. The gags
were slapstick and involved lots of horseplay, silly
faces, and falling down. And of course there was
the joke about the unicorn.

"Hey, Jessica," Mandy said, "did you see
what I just saw?"

"No, what did you just see, Mandy?" Jessica
asked.

"I just saw a unicorn walking down the
street," Mandy replied, pretending to be awe-
struck. "And it was wearing *two* pairs of purple
sneakers!" In the back row, Charlie Cashman guf-
fawed loudly.

Jessica looked blandly at Mandy. "What's so
weird about a unicorn wearing two pairs of purple
sneakers?" she asked. "Did you expect it to go
barefoot?"

The class was in an uproar, Mrs. Arnette

included. Even Lila and Ellen laughed, although their laughter sounded a bit forced.

But even though there was wild applause when their act was over, Jessica knew it hadn't been as good as it could have been. Unfortunately, Mandy's timing had been off and she had even forgotten one of her lines, something she had never done before. It hadn't really mattered, since Jessica had covered for her. But Jessica could tell that forgetting the line had bothered Mandy.

After class, when they were changing back into their clothes, Mandy said, "Thanks for covering for me. I hope I didn't mess things up too much."

Jessica shook her head. "I don't think anybody even noticed," she said. She looked closely at Mandy. "Is anything wrong, Mandy? Are you feeling OK?"

Mandy pulled off her wig and her long brown hair came tumbling down over her shoulders. "I'm OK," she said wearily. "Except that I've been tired for the past few days. Maybe I'm coming down with the flu. And that bump under my arm has been bothering me." She looked at Jessica. "Do you think we were good enough for an A?" she asked anxiously.

Jessica put her arm around Mandy's shoulders. "Are you kidding?" she asked. "We were *stars!* Boy, am I glad we got teamed up together."

"You bet!" Mandy's grin might have been a little shaky, but her voice was full of enthusiasm. "And who knows what's next? Hollywood, here we come!"

Five

On Monday, Jessica met Lila and Ellen in the hall
as she was going to social-studies class. They con-
gratulated her on her project.

"Everybody agreed that you and Mandy were
very funny," Lila said grudgingly. "Even the Hairnet liked your performance." She paused. "I do
think, though, that you overdid it just a little,
Jessica."

"Overdid it?" Jessica asked. "What do you
mean?"

"That joke about the unicorn, for instance,"
Ellen said, frowning slightly. "Couldn't you have
used another animal?"

Jessica tossed her head. "Maybe," she said.

"But I thought the unicorn was funny. As you said, everybody laughed, even the Hairnet."

Lila shrugged. "Well, it probably doesn't really matter," she said. "I'm sure nobody imagined you were making fun of the Unicorns. But you could have chosen some other color for the sneakers. Why did they have to be purple?"

"Because purple seemed funny," Jessica replied shortly.

"Well, you don't have to get mad about it," Ellen said.

"It was a good act, Jessica, and I have to compliment you and Mandy," Lila said soothingly. "Anyway, you must be relieved the project is over. Now you don't have to spend so much time with Mandy."

"Yes," Ellen agreed, "it must have been pretty awkward for you, after you gave her the news about our decision." She linked her arm in Jessica's. "Now you don't have to put up with her anymore."

Jessica pulled her arm away. "Listen, you guys, I've got to go," she said. "I don't want to be late to class. I'm on Mrs. Arnette's good side for a change, and I don't want to blow it."

Jessica wasn't really worried about being late to class. The truth was, she wanted to talk to Mandy. She had hoped they would get together over the weekend, and she'd been disappointed when she found out Mandy had to go visiting with her family instead.

When Jessica got to class, she was disappointed again. Mandy wasn't there. She brightened when Mrs. Arnette announced that she had selected two projects to be entered in the special school exhibition at the museum's 1920s festival. One was Jessica and Mandy's vaudeville act. The other was Elizabeth and Amy's videotape and report about the silent-film industry. The kids in the class applauded and Jessica felt very proud. Elizabeth and Amy were beaming.

Mrs. Arnette talked to Jessica after class. "Because your material is mostly original," she said, "I think you and Mandy stand a good chance of winning a prize. But you won't be able to enter your act live. Do you have the equipment to videotape it? I'd need the tape by this Friday in order to enter it in the exhibition."

Jessica nodded enthusiastically. "My parents have a video camera," she said. "I'm sure Mandy will be thrilled about this. I'll tell her tomorrow when she comes back to school."

But Mandy wasn't at school on Tuesday, either. That evening, Jessica decided to call her and tell her the good news about their act.

"Hi, Mandy," she said. "I've missed you. Have you been sick?"

"Hi, Jessica," Mandy said. Jessica thought she

sounded very tired. "I've had the flu or something. I had to stay in bed all weekend, and the last couple of days, too."

"All weekend?" Jessica asked sympathetically. "That's awful."

"Yes, it was," Mandy said. "I had to skip the visit to my relatives. But I'm better now, and Mom says I can go to school tomorrow. Has anything special happened while I've been gone?"

"Only the Hairnet's big announcement," Jessica said proudly. "She wants us to videotape our routine and enter the tape in the festival! But she's got to have the tape by Friday."

"That's terrific, Jessica!" Mandy exclaimed. "Do you know where we can borrow a video camera?"

"My dad's got one," Jessica told her. "And Elizabeth knows how to run it. Let's get together tomorrow and plan the taping."

"Great," Mandy said. "I'll see you in social studies, OK?"

But on Wednesday, Mandy's seat was still empty. Jessica went over to her twin's desk. "Have you heard anything about Mandy?" she asked. "I'm really getting worried."

Caroline Pearce walked by just in time to hear Jessica's question.

"You mean you haven't heard what happened to Mandy?" Caroline asked smugly.

Jessica turned to Caroline. "Happened to her? What are you talking about?"

"She was playing volleyball in gym class this morning when she fainted," Caroline reported. "I was standing right beside her when it happened."

"Oh, no! That sounds serious!" Elizabeth exclaimed.

"Ms. Langberg didn't think so," Caroline said. "We'd been running and it was hot in the gym. She said Mandy had been sick with the flu for the past few days and she was probably still weak. But Ms. Langberg sent her home anyway."

"I hope whatever she has isn't too bad," Jessica said anxiously. "This is the third day of school she's missed. And we only have two days left to get our videotape in."

"There's still plenty of time," Elizabeth reassured her. "You can tape it tomorrow after school."

When class was over, Mrs. Arnette asked Jessica to come to her desk.

"Jessica," she said, "Mandy Miller has missed several homework assignments. Could you take her work to her? And remember I have to have the videotape of your vaudeville routine by Friday."

Jessica shook her head. "If Mandy's sick, I'm not sure we can make the tape by the day after tomorrow. But we'll try."

Jessica worried about Mandy for the rest of the morning. She was still thinking about Mandy at lunch when Mary Wallace turned to her. "Did you hear about Mandy Miller getting sick in gym class?" Mary asked.

Jessica nodded. "Caroline Pearce told me."

"I hope she doesn't have anything contagious," Ellen said, frowning. "I sit next to her in math. I'd hate to catch something from her."

"It probably isn't very serious," Lila said casually. "Just the flu."

Jessica was about to argue that anything that made somebody faint was pretty serious when Janet Howell spoke up.

"Jessica," she said, "I don't think I've thanked you yet for taking care of Mandy Miller. Congratulations on a good job."

For a second, Jessica came close to yelling at Janet. None of the Unicorns had any idea how much Mandy had been hurt by the way they'd treated her, and they cared even less!

But Jessica restrained her temper. It was pointless to blame Janet or any of the other Unicorns for acting exactly the way they always acted. And anyway, they didn't know that Mandy was Jessica's friend. So Jessica steamed inside while several other unkind things were said about Mandy. As quickly as she could, she finished her lunch and left the table. She told her friends she was going to the library.

But as soon as Jessica was out of the cafeteria,

she headed for Mrs. Gerhart's classroom and got Mandy's home-ec assignment. Doing something to help Mandy made her feel a little better. Jessica had already asked her twin to get Mandy's English and math assignments, since the girls had those classes together. Elizabeth had also agreed to go with Jessica to Mandy's house after school.

The twins were just leaving school that afternoon with a folder full of Mandy's homework assignments when they ran into Lila and Ellen.

"Hi, Jessica," Lila called. "I'm glad we bumped into you. We can walk to Janet's together. There are one or two important things I've been meaning to talk to you about."

Jessica frowned. She had forgotten all about today's Unicorn meeting at Janet's house. "I'm afraid I can't make the meeting," Jessica said. "I've got something else I have to do."

Lila looked surprised. "What?" she asked.

Jessica tried to think of an excuse. She rarely missed a Unicorn meeting, and she probably should tell Lila why she was missing this one. But Lila and Ellen didn't know anything about her friendship with Mandy, and she wasn't ready to explain it to them. "Just something," she replied lamely.

"But this is a really important meeting, Jessica," Ellen insisted. "We're discussing our next

party, and Janet's giving out committee assignments."

"Tell Janet I'm sorry," Jessica said. She turned
to Elizabeth. "Come on, Elizabeth. We have to
go."

"Well, really, Jessica," Lila huffed. "I don't
know what Janet's going to say."

"I don't care what Janet says," Jessica muttered as she and Elizabeth hurried away.

Elizabeth looked closely at her sister. "I don't
think I've ever heard you talk like that to the Unicorns, Jess."

"That's because I've never been really angry
with them before," Jessica answered.

When they reached Mandy's house, Mrs.
Miller greeted the twins at the door. Jessica
thought she looked tired and worried, but her
voice sounded cheerful when she spoke.

"Hello, Jessica," she said. Then she looked
from Jessica to Elizabeth. "Oh, my," she said.
"There are *two* of you."

"This is my sister, Elizabeth," Jessica said.
"We've brought Mandy her homework, and I'd
like to talk to her about making the videotape of
our vaudeville act. How is she? Can we come in
and see her for a little while?"

Mrs. Miller's face seemed to tighten. "I'm
sorry, Jessica," she said. "I know that Mandy
would like to see you. But the doctor says she

can't have any company for at least the rest of this week."

Jessica couldn't believe what she was hearing. "It sounds as if she's pretty sick."

"It's difficult to say just what's wrong, Jessica," Mrs. Miller explained. "Mandy went to the hospital this afternoon to have some tests done. We'll have to wait and see what the results are."

"Does that mean Mandy won't be able to make the videotape?" Elizabeth asked.

"Mrs. Arnette says if we're going to enter our project in the festival exhibition," Jessica added, "we have to turn it in *this* Friday."

"I'm afraid that making the video is out of the question," Mrs. Miller said regretfully. "Mandy has to stay in bed. She needs a lot of rest."

Jessica sighed. "Well, if there's anything we can do to help, please let us know." She handed Mrs. Miller the folder full of Mandy's homework. "And tell Mandy we miss her and want her to get well really soon."

"I will, Jessica." Mrs. Miller blinked as if she were trying not to cry. "It'll cheer Mandy up to know you stopped by."

"I'm really sorry about your project, Jessica," Elizabeth said as they started home.

"I am, too," Jessica said. "It would have been fun to make the videotape with Mandy. And I think we had a good chance at winning. But I'm more upset about Mandy than I am about our project. What do you think is wrong with her?"

Elizabeth shook her head. "I don't know," she said. "Did she tell you how she was feeling?"

Jessica frowned. "Yes. Last Friday after our act she said she'd been really tired lately. She thought she had the flu, and she was complaining about a bump under her arm that was bothering her."

"A bump under her arm?" Elizabeth asked.

"The day we did our dress rehearsal, we got into a tug-of-war over a feather boa," Jessica said. She couldn't help but feel a little guilty as she remembered what had happened. "The boa tore, and I went in one direction and Mandy went in another. She hit her ribs, and she got a bump under her arm." She turned to Elizabeth. Suddenly it occurred to her that *she* might be responsible for whatever was making Mandy sick. "You don't think she hurt herself when she fell, do you? Is that why she's sick?"

"I don't see how a fall could have had anything to do with the flu, Jess," Elizabeth said reassuringly. "Mrs. Miller said Mandy's doctors had run some tests. I'm sure the results will tell them what's wrong."

"I hope so," Jessica said sadly. "I really miss Mandy."

*   *   *

On Thursday, Jessica told Mrs. Arnette she and Mandy couldn't make their videotape together.

"I'm sorry, Jessica," Mrs. Arnette said sympathetically. "You two did a very good job and I think it had an excellent chance of winning a prize in the special school exhibition." Mrs. Arnette paused thoughtfully. "I wonder . . . I know it's short notice, but what would you think of substituting another person for Mandy in the act?"

Jessica frowned. "Another person? But Mandy wrote most of the material and supplied all the costumes. They belonged to her grandparents. It wouldn't be right to let somebody else take the credit for Mandy's work."

"I understand," Mrs. Arnette said. "But you might ask Mandy how she feels about it. Of course, because the act was Mandy's idea, her name would appear on the entry form, along with yours and that of the person who took her place."

"But who could we find to substitute for her?" Jessica asked. "There isn't anybody else like Mandy."

"That's true," Mrs. Arnette agreed kindly. "But how about Elizabeth? Mandy's costume would fit her, and I'm sure she could learn Mandy's lines. And since you're twins you would certainly make a memorable pair."

Jessica nodded. Elizabeth would be a good choice. Then she frowned. "But Elizabeth is entering *her* project," she said. "And anyway, I really don't think we could turn in the tape by tomorrow. Even if Elizabeth would take Mandy's place, she wouldn't have time to learn her lines by tonight."

"I don't think there's any problem with Elizabeth standing in for Mandy, even though she's involved with another project," Mrs. Arnette replied. "And I'll try to arrange for a late entry. Do you suppose you could submit the tape by Monday?"

"Maybe," Jessica said. "I'll talk to Mandy about it. She can't have any company, but her mother didn't say anything about not taking any telephone calls. If she agrees, I'll ask Elizabeth. And I'll let you know tomorrow."

"Good luck," Mrs. Arnette said.

That evening Jessica called Mandy. Mrs. Miller answered and explained that Mandy was too tired to come to the phone. But she agreed to give Mandy Jessica's message, and a few minutes later Mrs. Miller called back to say that Mandy thought it would be a wonderful idea for Elizabeth to take her place. Jessica could stop by the house after school on Friday to borrow Mandy's costume and get the props.

"Oh, and one more thing," Mrs. Miller added. "Mandy said to break a leg!"

"Break a leg?" Jessica asked blankly. Then she remembered the phrase was an old show-business way of saying *good luck*, and she laughed. "Tell her thanks," she said. "And tell her I miss her."

"I will," Mrs. Miller promised warmly.

On Friday Jessica picked up Mandy's costume and the props. On Saturday, she and Elizabeth worked almost nonstop on the routine, practicing their lines and perfecting their timing. When they were sure they had it right, Mr. Wakefield made the video. The entire Wakefield family watched it that evening.

"What do you think, Mom?" Elizabeth asked when the tape was over. "Is it good enough to enter in the festival exhibition?"

"I think it's very good, girls," Mrs. Wakefield said. "You're really funny."

"Not bad at all, squirts," Steven remarked. He chuckled. "My favorite is the joke about the unicorn in the purple sneakers. Where'd you get that one?"

"We didn't get it anywhere," Jessica replied. "Mandy made it up. All our material is original, except for the Abbott and Costello routine."

"Well, I think 'it's a take,' as they say in the movies," Mr. Wakefield said.

"I do, too." Jessica smiled. "Can we make a

copy of the tape to keep? I'd like Mandy to see it. The Millers don't have a VCR, but we could loan them ours. Or maybe when Mandy's better she could come over here and watch it."

"I think that's a very good idea," Mrs. Wakefield said approvingly.

On Monday, Mandy was still absent from school. Jessica and Elizabeth gave their videotape to Mrs. Arnette. She had checked with the exhibition organizers and they had agreed to accept the late entry.

Jessica wanted to go to Mandy's house after school to see how she was feeling, but Lila insisted Jessica go to the Fowlers' for dinner.

"I don't know where you've been keeping yourself for the past week, Jessica," Lila scolded her. "You haven't spent *any* time at all with your friends. I'm beginning to wonder if you're still interested in the Unicorns."

Jessica sighed. Lila had a point. She'd been so busy with Mandy and their project that she'd missed several Unicorn meetings. Jessica agreed to go to Lila's for dinner that evening. She told herself that Mandy would surely be back at school the next day.

Late that afternoon, just as Jessica was ready to leave for the Fowlers', the phone rang. It was Mrs. Miller.

"Hello, Jessica," she said. She sounded

weary. "Mandy would like you to come over and visit with her for a little while. Do you think you could stop by today?"

"I don't know. I'm supposed to be somewhere for dinner," Jessica answered. "I was just leaving."

"Please, dear. You don't have to stay long," Mrs. Miller urged. "Perhaps you could delay your dinner? Mandy still isn't supposed to have company, but she very much wants to see you. It's important."

Jessica frowned. There was something about Mrs. Miller's tone that bothered her. "Is something wrong?" she asked fearfully.

"It might be a good idea if I talked to your mother, dear," Mrs. Miller said evasively. "Is she there?"

"I'll get her," Jessica said. There was a cold lump in her stomach. What was going on? She called her mother to the phone. Then she went upstairs to find Elizabeth, who was in her bedroom doing homework.

"Elizabeth," she said, "Mandy wants me to come over for a little while. Could you come with me?"

"Now?" Elizabeth asked in surprise. She glanced at the clock. "It's almost dinnertime. Besides, I thought you were going to Lila's."

"I know," Jessica said. "I will go to Lila's, but

I can't think about that now. Oh, Lizzie," she burst out, "I have the most awful feeling! Mrs. Miller sounded so strange. I think there's something terribly wrong with Mandy! I need you to come with me for moral support. I don't think Mandy is allowed to see too many people at a time, so you'll probably have to wait in the van, but *please* come anyway."

Elizabeth looked at Jessica's worried face and closed her book. "Of course I will," she said. "Let's go."

While Mrs. Wakefield and Elizabeth went out to the van, Jessica made a hurried telephone call to Lila. She didn't want to tell Lila where she was going, so she just said that she had to stop somewhere with her mother and that she'd be at Lila's house as soon as she could.

Lila demanded to know where they were going.

"I . . . I can't tell you," Jessica answered bluntly.

"I wish you'd stop being so mysterious about everything these days, Jessica Wakefield," Lila said frostily. "If this is some kind of game you're playing, I don't think it's any fun." And she slammed down the receiver.

At that moment, Jessica didn't care whether or not Lila was mad at her. The drive to the Millers' house seemed endless. Her mother didn't talk, Elizabeth was silent, and Jessica was too anxious to say a word. Her heart pounded, the palms of her hands were sweaty, and she was filled with a growing dread.

Something was terribly, frighteningly wrong with Mandy, she just knew it. But what?

Six

◇

At last the van reached Mandy's house. Mrs. Miller invited Jessica inside, while Mrs. Wakefield and Elizabeth waited in the van. Mrs. Miller's face was strained and she looked very tired. Jessica headed straight upstairs.

Mandy was in bed in the room she shared with Cecilia. Jessica had never seen Mandy look so awful. Her cheeks were drawn and pale and she looked as if she'd lost weight. But when she spoke, she sounded almost like her normal, happy self.

"So," she said, tossing her head, "I hear you've replaced me in our act."

"I hope you don't mind," Jessica said guiltily. "Elizabeth said to tell you she knows she's not half as funny as you are. But it was the only way our act could be in the exhibition.''

Mandy grinned. ''Of course I don't mind, silly,'' she said. ''What did I tell you? Hollywood, here we come! Just be sure you split the prize with me, OK?''

''The prize?'' Jessica asked blankly.

''Of course, the prize. What is it? A tour through one of the movie lots? A hot date with Nick England?''

Jessica laughed. She hadn't even thought to ask Mrs. Arnette about the prizes! ''I'll find out and let you know,'' she promised. ''And when you're better, you can come over to our house and watch the tape on our VCR.'' Jessica paused. ''Your mom said you wanted to talk to me about something.''

Mandy nodded and pushed herself up against the pillow. ''I went to the hospital last week. The doctors ran a bunch of tests.''

''Yes, I know,'' Jessica said. ''Your mom told me. Have they found anything yet?''

''Funny you should ask,'' Mandy replied. She looked at her hands. ''We just got the results today. It seems I didn't have the flu after all. False alarm.''

''You didn't?'' Jessica asked. ''If it wasn't the flu, what was it?''

Mandy leaned forward and grinned. ''I tell

you, Jessica," she said, "the Unicorns are going to turn absolutely green when they hear what I've got. I am going to get so much attention from everybody, they're going to wish they had let me into the club after all." Her grin faded a bit. "What I've got is cancer."

Jessica's heart seemed to stop. After a long moment she whispered, *"Cancer?"*

Mandy leaned back against the pillow. "Yeah. That's what the tests showed."

Jessica was at a loss for words. She was horrified and sad and confused, all at the same time. She had no idea of what she was supposed to say. *I'm sorry* sounded so poor and thin, and *I hope you get better soon* was what you said when somebody had a cold or the measles. People who got cancer didn't always get better. Her heart was thudding slowly and painfully in her chest. Was Mandy going to *die*?

As if she had read Jessica's mind, Mandy reached out and grabbed her hand. "Hey, Jess, it's OK! Don't look so scared. I'm not going to die. At least, I'm not planning to." She squeezed Jessica's hand. "I've got too many things to do."

Jessica tried to say something, but her tongue seemed stuck to the roof of her mouth.

"Anyway," Mandy went on carelessly, "lots of people get cancer these days without dying. There are all kinds of successful treatments, you know. Surgery and radiation treatment and chemotherapy—all kinds of stuff. And I've got a terrific doctor." She rolled her eyes dramatically. "You should see him. He looks just like Kent Kellerman, the TV star. He is *so* cute. I'll bet Lila would give up her best purple sweater for a chance to let him take her pulse."

Jessica knew Mandy was trying to make her feel better, but she still felt terrible. She was remembering all the horrible things she'd read and heard about cancer, and a dozen questions were crowding into her mind.

"Are you going to lose all your hair?" she blurted out. When she saw the stunned look on Mandy's face, she wanted to cry. What a stupid thing to say! How could she have been so thoughtless?

Mandy was silent for a few seconds. Then she burst into laughter. "Don't worry, Jess. I know you didn't mean to upset me."

"I spoke before I thought," Jessica said regretfully. "I'm always doing it, Mandy. I'm such a jerk. I'm sorry."

"Don't be sorry," Mandy said, still smiling. "This is the first time I've laughed in a whole miserable week. You're good for me, Jessica."

Suddenly, Mandy leaned back against the pillow. Her face was gray. Jessica realized how weak Mandy must be, and she was scared.

"Sorry, Jess," Mandy said quietly. She closed her eyes. "All those tests, a whole week in and out of the hospital—it really wore me out. And now I've got to go back and have surgery."

Jessica stood up. "It's time for me to go anyway," she said.

Mandy's eyes popped open. "Let me know what happens with our project," she commanded in a stronger voice. "And tell Elizabeth I'm really glad she could join our act. Temporarily, of course. In a few weeks, I'll be back, better than ever."

"I'll tell her," Jessica promised. "Good luck with your surgery, Mandy."

Mandy nodded. "Thanks. Oh, and I wanted to let you know something else. It's OK to tell people. About what I have, I mean." She grinned a little. "If you don't want to tell everyone yourself, just tell Caroline Pearce. She'll be glad to spread the word."

Jessica nodded and turned toward the door. "Break a leg, Mandy."

"Yeah," Mandy mumbled, closing her eyes again. "Same to you, Jess."

By the time Jessica got out to the van, where Elizabeth and Mrs. Wakefield were waiting, she was blinded by tears.

"Are you OK, Jessica?" Elizabeth asked anxiously.

"Mandy's got cancer!" Jessica cried.

Elizabeth put her arms around Jessica while Mrs. Wakefield started the van. "I know," she whispered. "Mom told me while you were inside. Oh, Jess, it's awful!"

For a moment, Jessica could only cry. Elizabeth held her and stroked her hair. Finally, when Jessica managed to calm down a little, she blew her nose.

"Mom," she said, "did Mrs. Miller tell you?"

"Yes," Mrs. Wakefield said, "when we talked on the phone earlier. I'm very sorry, Jessica."

Jessica bit her lip. "You've got to tell me the truth, Mom," she said. "Is Mandy going to die?"

Mrs. Wakefield was silent for a moment, her eyes fixed on the road. Then she said, "The cancer Mandy has is something called non-Hodgkin's lymphoma, Jessica."

"Non-Hodgkin's lymphoma," Jessica repeated slowly so that she would remember the words. "What does that mean?"

"That's a name for a bad growth that's appeared in a lymph gland," Mrs. Wakefield replied. "Everybody has several lymph glands. One of them is under the arm. That's where Mandy's cancer has appeared."

"Oh," Jessica said. She remembered the lump Mandy had found when she fell over the trunk.

"If the growth is only in that one gland,"

Mrs. Wakefield went on, "Mandy will be in good shape. But the growth can spread. Only surgery can tell where the growth is located just now."

"I see," Jessica said.

"Mrs. Miller said Mandy's going to have surgery Friday morning," Mrs. Wakefield added. "Depending on what the doctors find, she may have to undergo radiation treatment or chemotherapy to wipe out any remaining cancer cells in her body."

"But what happens if they don't get it all?" Jessica asked worriedly. "What happens if the cancer spreads?"

Mrs. Wakefield turned the corner onto their street and pulled into the drive before she answered. Then she turned to face Jessica and Elizabeth.

"Twenty-five years ago, Mandy's future would have been very sad," she said quietly. "But now, doctors have learned how to treat this disease. Mandy's chances are excellent. I can't tell you there's nothing to worry about. But Mrs. Miller says Mandy's doctor is optimistic."

Jessica smiled a little. "Yes, Mandy mentioned her doctor."

Then all of a sudden Jessica found herself crying again, and she couldn't stop. Her mother's explanation sounded very reasonable and reassuring. Doctors could do things now they couldn't do only a few years ago. But Jessica couldn't ignore the awful fear that rose up in her when she thought about Mandy's cancer—and the chance that Mandy might die.

Seven

◇

Jessica didn't go to Lila's house that night for dinner. Instead, Mrs. Wakefield phoned Lila and told her Jessica didn't feel well.

On Tuesday morning Lila was waiting by Jessica's locker. "You couldn't have been *too* sick last night," she said sharply. "You look just fine this morning."

Jessica took her English book from the locker shelf. "I wasn't sick last night," she replied.

Lila put her hands on her hips. "Then what was wrong with you?" she demanded. "Your mother said you didn't feel up to coming over."

"I went to see Mandy Miller," Jessica said.

"What?" Lila exclaimed angrily. "But you were supposed to come to *my* house, Jessica!

What's this thing you have about Mandy, anyway? She may have everybody rolling in the aisles with her comic routines, but she's still a weirdo. If you keep hanging around with her, you may not have any other friends left."

Jessica looked calmly at Lila. "Mandy has cancer," she said quietly.

Lila's eyes widened and her mouth dropped open. "Cancer?" she squeaked. "You're kidding."

Jessica shook her head. "It's a cancer of the lymph glands. She's having surgery on Friday."

Caroline Pearce was walking past them as Jessica spoke. She stopped, her eyes bright with curiosity. "Surgery? Who's having surgery?"

"Mandy Miller," Lila answered. "She has cancer."

"Cancer!" Caroline exclaimed. "I don't believe it."

"Well, it's true," Lila said importantly. "Now, if you'll excuse me, I have to go tell Janet."

Jessica frowned. "Janet?" she asked. "But Janet isn't a friend of Mandy's. Why would she be interested?"

"You know Janet," Lila said. "She'd be really mad at me if I didn't tell her something this important right away."

Jessica sighed resignedly. Lila was right. "I'll go with you," she said.

"No!" Lila exclaimed. Then, in a softer voice,

she said, "That's OK, Jessica. Janet probably won't be interested in the details." She turned and hurried off.

Jessica stared after Lila. That was odd. She had the feeling Lila didn't want her to talk to Janet about Mandy. Then she noticed Caroline still tugging at her arm.

"You can tell *me* the details, Jessica," she said eagerly. "I'm interested!"

Jessica remembered what Mandy had said about Caroline being eager to spread the word about Mandy's illness. She almost smiled as she told Caroline everything she knew.

By lunchtime, Caroline had done her job. All the students at Sweet Valley Middle School knew that Mandy Miller had cancer. Everybody wanted to talk about it and kids kept pestering Jessica about it. She did her best to answer everybody's questions briefly and accurately without embroidering any of the details.

Jessica noticed that nobody came right out and asked if Mandy was going to die. But she had the feeling that was what everybody wanted to know. So she told them exactly what her mother had told her: that Mandy's chances for recovery were good as long as the cancer hadn't spread.

To Jessica's surprise, the Unicorns never mentioned Mandy's name during lunch. Instead, they talked about the party they were planning, gossiped about boys, and got into an argument about whether Lila ought to buy a new purple sweater or a pair of purple suede ankle boots. Most of the Unicorns were in favor of the purple boots.

At first, Jessica was relieved that no one asked her about Mandy. And it was nice to drift along with the Unicorns' chitchat, even if it did seem sillier than usual.

But after a while, Jessica's relief turned to anger. Janet and Lila knew what was happening with Mandy, and she was sure that by now all the other Unicorns knew, too. They couldn't help but know. Everybody at school did. So why were they avoiding the subject? Weren't they even a little bit interested in the fact that Mandy had cancer? Didn't they care that she might die?

By the time lunch was over, Jessica was steaming. Elizabeth had been right all along when she had said the Unicorns were self-centered and snobbish. Not only were they snobs, Jessica decided, they were heartless, too. She stumbled away from the table, feeling worse than she'd ever felt in her life.

Halfway across the cafeteria, Ellen caught up with her. "Jessica," she said, "you ran off before we could tell you that a bunch of us are going to the Dairi Burger this afternoon to talk about the party. Meet us by Janet's locker after school, and we'll all walk together."

Jessica shook her head. "No," she said. She didn't even try to make an excuse.

Ellen looked at her closely and frowned. "You aren't mad at us, are you, Jessica? You're acting awfully weird."

Jessica hesitated. She could tell Ellen how she felt about the way the Unicorns were behaving. But what good would it do? Nothing would change. The Unicorns would just go on being Unicorns, forever and ever. She shook her head and turned away.

"Jessica, what's wrong?" Ellen called after her. "You can tell me."

Jessica didn't turn around. It was useless to talk to Ellen. Ellen wouldn't understand. There was nobody she could tell about the angry, sad, scared feelings that were tumbling around inside of her—except Elizabeth.

Right after school, Jessica went in search of her twin. She found her in the *Sixers* room, working on the next issue of the newspaper. "Lizzie," she asked, "do you think we could, well, maybe go to the park? I . . . I need somebody to talk to."

Elizabeth put down the article she was editing. "Of course," she said sympathetically. "But I'm waiting for Julie Porter to bring in an article. Do you mind hanging around for a few minutes?"

Jessica shook her head. "I've got to get something out of my locker, anyway. See you in a little bit.''

As Jessica turned the corner toward her locker, she bumped into Julie Porter.

"Hi, Jessica,'' Julie said. "Hey, that was a pretty neat thing for you guys to do. Sending those flowers, I mean.''

"Flowers?'' Jessica asked in surprise. "What flowers?''

Julie frowned. "You don't know? I heard the Unicorns signed a get-well card, too. I just assumed it was all your idea.''

"Julie,'' Jessica said firmly, "will you please tell me what you're talking about?''

"I'm talking about the flowers and the card the Unicorns sent to Mandy Miller,'' Julie explained. "I was surprised because Caroline Pearce told me the Unicorns had just turned Mandy down for membership.'' She looked curiously at Jessica. "You mean it wasn't your idea? You didn't sign the card?''

Wordlessly, Jessica shook her head. She couldn't imagine why the Unicorns hadn't asked her to sign the card. Had they just forgotten to include her? Or had they deliberately excluded her? She remembered the conversation at lunch. Not one Unicorn had even mentioned Mandy. What was going on?

Jessica was still puzzling over the Unicorns'

behavior when Elizabeth met her in the hall. They started for the park.

"Julie just told me the Unicorns sent flowers to Mandy," Elizabeth remarked. "That was nice of them."

"Well, maybe," Jessica replied. "Or maybe it's like the time Amy's house burned down and the Unicorns wanted to be friends with her just to be part of the excitement."

"Yes, I've noticed that when something big happens, the Unicorns like to take part of the credit or steal some of the limelight," Elizabeth said. "Julie also told me you didn't know about the flowers, Jess," she added.

Jessica nodded glumly. "Nobody told me about it, Elizabeth. In fact, when I was with the Unicorns at lunch, they acted as if Mandy didn't exist. I know the Unicorns must be dying of curiosity, but not one of them has asked me a single question about Mandy. Except for Lila, this morning."

"But why?" Elizabeth asked. "Don't they know you two are good friends?"

"No, they don't," Jessica answered. "But that's no reason to leave me out of doing something nice for Mandy. Ellen's not a good friend of Mandy's, either, but I'll bet she was asked to sign the card." The girls reached the park and sat down on a bench. "But the Unicorns are the least of what's bothering me, Elizabeth," Jessica said unhappily.

Elizabeth picked up a leaf and twirled it around in her fingers. "I know how you're feeling," she said. "You think if you just keep denying this, maybe it won't be true."

"That's it exactly," Jessica agreed. "And there's so much I don't know and I feel so dumb about asking. Like, is the cancer contagious? Is it something I can catch from Mandy?"

"The answer to that is no." Brooke Dennis came around from behind the bench. "Sorry. I couldn't help overhearing. Cancer isn't contagious." Amy Sutton was with Brooke. They were carrying their tennis rackets, and Amy was holding a tennis ball. "I know because my cousin had cancer a few years ago," Brooke added.

"Did she . . . is she all right now?" Jessica asked hesitantly. She was afraid of the answer.

Brooke nodded as she and Amy sat down on the grass in front of the bench. "Yes," she said, "she's fine. But when she first got sick, I was really scared. I was afraid that she was going to die. I was afraid I might get sick, too, because I'd spent a few weeks at her house. But her doctor explained that cancer isn't like a cold. It isn't something you catch from other people."

"Well," Amy asked curiously, "how *do* you get it?"

"I've been wondering about that, too," Jessica said. She laced her fingers together and looked down at them. "You see, Mandy and I were clowning around last week, and she fell over an old trunk. That's when she found the lump under her arm." She swallowed. "Is cancer something you get by hurting yourself?" This was the really scary question, the one that had been on Jessica's mind ever since she had seen Mandy the night before. Jessica was the one who had been tugging on the other end of the pink feather boa. If Mandy's cancer was the result of the fall, was it all Jessica's fault?

Brooke shook her head. "I'm no expert. But the way I understand it, cancer *makes* a lump, it isn't *caused* by a lump. Mandy's cancer didn't come from falling down and hurting herself."

Jessica breathed a sigh of relief. At least she didn't have to go around with a guilty conscience.

"What happened to your cousin when she found out she was sick?" Elizabeth asked. "Was she out of school for a long time?"

"Not that long a time," Brooke replied. "She was absent for a few weeks. But she missed some days over the next several months because she had to undergo radiation therapy every so often. And her hair fell out."

Jessica gulped. What an awful thing, to lose your hair! Somehow that almost seemed worse than having cancer. She closed her eyes for a moment and tried to imagine Mandy without the thick, glossy brown hair that hung down to her waist. But she couldn't.

"Gosh," Amy said, feeling her own blond hair, "that would be pretty awful, being bald." She paused. "I wonder how I'd feel if I got cancer? Would I be the type to cry all the time and make people feel sorry for me? Or would I be the brave type, a real inspiration to my family and friends?"

Brooke laughed teasingly. "If you ask me, Amy, you'd act as if nothing had happened. You'd be playing tennis right up to the very last minute before they dragged you off to surgery. And you'd be really mad if anybody felt sorry for you."

Jessica touched her own hair, not wanting to imagine what she would do if it were *she* who had cancer. She couldn't imagine undergoing a treatment that would make her lose all her hair. She would want to stay in the house until it grew back. Then her eyes widened and she sucked in her breath. *Would* it grow back?

As if she'd read Jessica's mind, Elizabeth asked, "What did your cousin do after she lost her hair, Brooke?"

"She got a wig," Brooke said. "It was a really pretty one, too. It looked a lot like her own hair. If she didn't tell you she was wearing a wig, you'd probably never know. But it cost a lot of money. Good wigs are expensive. The cheap ones don't look very natural."

"Did her own hair grow back?" Jessica asked nervously.

"Yes," Brooke said, "when the chemotherapy and radiation therapy ended. Now her hair is as pretty as it was before."

"I wish I could visit Mandy," Amy said thoughtfully. "But it's probably just as well I can't. I wouldn't know what to say to her." She shook her head. "I don't know how to treat somebody who's got cancer. I want to help, but I don't know what to do."

"I guess all we can do is be Mandy's friends and let her talk about the way she feels," Elizabeth said.

"Elizabeth's right," Brooke agreed. "We shouldn't treat Mandy any differently than we did before. When my cousin got cancer, some kids who had never paid any attention to her suddenly made a big fuss over her. She thought it was pretty funny."

"Tell that to the Unicorns," Amy remarked with a sarcastic laugh. "Last week they thought Mandy was a big nuisance and they couldn't get rid of her fast enough. Now I hear they sent her a big bunch of flowers. How hypocritical can you get?" Then she looked at Jessica. "Oops, sorry,

Jessica. But you know how I feel about the way the Unicorns act sometimes."

Jessica usually defended the Unicorns. But today she found herself agreeing with Amy, although she didn't admit it out loud. "I didn't have anything to do with sending flowers to Mandy," was all she said.

"You didn't?" Brooke asked. "I thought you organized it. After all, you and Mandy were partners in the social-studies project."

"Maybe they just couldn't find you when they signed the card," Amy suggested.

"Maybe," Jessica said. She had a feeling, though, that the Unicorns had left her out on purpose. But why?

Brooke glanced at her watch. "Hey, Amy, if we don't hurry we're going to lose the court we signed up for."

Amy got to her feet. "If you talk to Mandy," she said to Jessica, "tell her I said to get well soon."

"Me, too," Brooke said. "Tell her we miss her."

"If I talk to her, I will," Jessica promised.

The twins sat for a few moments in silence after Brooke and Amy ran off. All around them were the ordinary sounds of the park—kids laughing, the *slap-slap* of tennis balls, the tinny merry-go-round music from the ice-cream cart.

But to Jessica, it didn't feel like an ordinary day. The sadness and fear whirling around inside her made ordinary things look and sound very different.

Jessica sighed. "I've been wondering," she said thoughtfully, "why this had to happen to Mandy. Of all the people I know, she's the most cheerful, and the nicest."

"I've been wondering the same thing," Elizabeth replied. "Why Mandy? Why not me? Or Brooke, or Amy?"

"Or Lila or Ellen or Janet?" Jessica said sadly. "They're the ones who hurt Mandy, when all she wanted was their friendship. Or why not *me?* I wasn't very nice to Mandy, either." She shook her head. "Mandy doesn't deserve to have cancer. Isn't there any justice in the world?"

Elizabeth reached for Jessica's hand. "I guess that's just one of those questions we'll never know the answer to, Jess."

"I guess," Jessica agreed sadly. "But that won't keep me from asking it."

For the rest of the day, and every day for the rest of the week, the question ran through Jessica's mind. Why did it have to be *Mandy?*

Eight

◇

On Friday, Jessica walked home with Elizabeth and Amy. They were talking about Mandy and wondering how her surgery had gone. It had been scheduled for that morning. Jessica hadn't thought of anything else all day.

"I heard Janet and Lila sent Mandy some perfume," Amy remarked. "Ellen sent her a huge box of fancy Swiss chocolates, and Kimberly Haver and Betsy Gordon pooled their money and got her a big glass pig full of jelly beans."

Jessica had managed to avoid the Unicorns for most of the week, so she hadn't heard anything about their presents to Mandy. And not one of them had telephoned her, not even to ask why she had missed the regular weekly meeting. They seemed to be avoiding her, just as she was avoiding them. But being left out didn't hurt as much as it would have under other circumstances. Jessica was so worried about Mandy that everything else, including the Unicorns, seemed unimportant.

Elizabeth laughed. "Mandy has gotten so many goodies that she'll be a blimp by the time she gets back to school! Jessica and I baked a batch of her favorite chocolate-chip cookies and took them over to her house the other day."

"If Mandy can't eat everything, Archie, Mandy's little brother, will be glad to help," Jessica said. "He's even worse than Steven when it comes to raiding the refrigerator. Mandy's always complaining about what a pest he is."

Amy grinned. "Maybe Mandy would loan him to me for a little while. Being an only child isn't always that much fun."

Elizabeth nodded thoughtfully. "Sometimes I envy Belinda Layton. She's got such a cute baby brother. I wouldn't mind having a new little brother myself."

"Make that a sister," Jessica said emphatically. She shuddered. "Archie collects lizards and snakes. Sometimes they wind up in the bathtub."

Amy laughed. "Maybe being an only child isn't that bad after all. At least I know I'm not going to find a snake in the bathtub." They had come to Amy's corner, just a block from the Wakefield house. "Call me as soon as you find out how Mandy's surgery went," Amy said as she turned to walk down her street.

"We will," Jessica promised. "We might not hear anything until tomorrow, though."

But Jessica was wrong. She and Elizabeth were just walking in the door as Mrs. Wakefield hung up the phone. "That was Mrs. Miller," she said brightly. "Mandy came through her surgery beautifully. She's going to be fine!"

Jessica flung her arms around her mother. "That's great!" she cried joyfully. "Oh, Mom, that's wonderful news!"

"It *is* good news," Mrs. Wakefield said happily. "Mandy's cancer hadn't spread beyond the original site of the lump. Her doctor says she's got an excellent chance for a complete recovery."

"Will she have to have radiation treatment or chemotherapy?" Elizabeth asked.

"Yes, as a precautionary measure," Mrs. Wakefield replied. "Her doctor wants to make sure all the cancer cells are killed."

Jessica was silent for a moment. "Will she lose her hair right away?" she asked at last.

"Maybe she won't lose it at all," Elizabeth suggested hopefully. "Is that possible, Mom?"

Mrs. Wakefield put her arms around the twins' shoulders. "Cancer therapy isn't a very pleasant thing," she said in reply to their questions. "The radiation bombards healthy cells as well as cancer cells. Often it makes people feel even worse than they did before the treatment, at least for a little while. It's very likely that Mandy will lose her hair, girls."

Jessica had thought the awful, suspenseful waiting would be over when Mandy came through the surgery and was on the way to recovery. But now there was a new worry. How would Mandy feel when she lost her hair, the long, lovely hair she prized so much?

On Monday morning, Lila and Ellen were waiting by Jessica's locker to tell her that Janet was concerned about the meetings she had missed. At lunchtime, Janet herself was waiting for Jessica at the cafeteria door, and when she came along, Janet gave her a special smile.

"I've been very worried about you lately, Jessica," she said.

Jessica wanted to tell Janet that the person she should really be worried about was Mandy. But Janet had a sharp tongue, and Jessica didn't have any desire to be the target of it. "I've been kind of busy," was all she said.

"I understand," Janet replied. "But we need you to help us get ready for our party." She leaned forward. "I want you to be in charge of the decorations, Jessica. You have such a good eye for color and such a good sense of organization. Nobody else can do the job as well as you can."

Jessica couldn't help but feel flattered. The decorations were always a very important aspect of the Unicorns' parties. It was an honor to have Janet ask her to be in charge. Still, Jessica was pretty upset about the way the Unicorns had acted toward Mandy, first using her to do their errands, then rejecting her, now showering her with flowers and presents. And lately, Jessica had also been upset about the way the Unicorns had been behaving toward Jessica herself. What were they up to, anyway?

"Well . . ." she said thoughtfully.

Janet looked closely at Jessica. "You're a very valuable member of the Unicorns, Jessica. I'd hate it if anything came between you and our club."

Jessica thought. It wouldn't help Mandy if she continued to be cool toward the Unicorns. Besides, if she stopped hanging around with the Unicorns, who would she hang around with? They were making an effort to be friendly again. Maybe the best thing was to pretend nothing had ever happened.

"Thank you, Janet," she said, smiling. "I'll be glad to be in charge of the decorations."

"Good," Janet said. "Now, let's get some lunch, OK? Lila, Ellen, and the others are waiting for us."

"Yes, let's," Jessica said happily. It felt very good to have things between her and her friends almost back to normal again—almost. Jessica still found herself wondering why not one Unicorn had said a word in her presence about sending flowers and presents to Mandy, or asked about Mandy's surgery, or wondered aloud when she would be back at school. In fact, no one even mentioned Mandy's name. Of course, in one way Jessica was relieved. Their silence meant she didn't have to pretend she and Mandy weren't friends when they really were.

Thursday evening when Jessica got home, she learned that Mrs. Miller had called to say Mandy could have visitors again. It was an invitation Jessica had been waiting for eagerly. So on Friday afternoon she hurried to her locker after her final class, and then set out for Mandy's house. She was hoping she wouldn't run into a Unicorn, who might ask her where she was going. And for once she didn't see a single one of her friends as she ran through the hall. But she did bump into Mrs. Arnette.

"Jessica!" Mrs. Arnette exclaimed. "I'm so glad I caught you before you left for the weekend. I've been looking for you."

"You have?" Jessica asked apprehensively.

What did Mrs. Arnette want? Had she done something wrong?

Mrs. Arnette was smiling broadly. "I just received a phone call from the organizers of the 1920s festival," she said. "Your social-studies project has been awarded first place among all the middle-school entries! And Elizabeth and Amy's has won second place!"

Jessica's mouth dropped open. In all her worry over Mandy's surgery, she had completely forgotten about the festival exhibition. "First place?" she squeaked. "We won *first place?*"

"And that's not all," Mrs. Arnette continued. "The contest officials would like you and Elizabeth to perform your act *live* at the museum in Hollywood!"

"Perform? In Hollywood?" Jessica couldn't believe what she was hearing. "When do they want us to perform?" she asked. "Could we delay the performance until Mandy's well enough to be in the act again?"

Mrs. Arnette shook her head regretfully. "I'm afraid not, Jessica. They'd like to schedule your skit for a week from Saturday, the day they're sponsoring a program of silent films. I doubt Mandy would be up to performing so soon after her surgery."

Jessica nodded sadly. "But I know she'll be glad to hear that we won first place," she said brightly. "What's the prize?" she asked. "Mandy will want to know."

Mrs. Arnette sighed happily. "It's a wonderful prize, Jessica. You'll be thrilled."

"That's great!" Jessica exclaimed. "Is it a trip somewhere?"

"Oh, much better than that." Mrs. Arnette clasped her hands. "It's a computer!"

"A computer!" Jessica was disappointed. She wasn't very interested in computers, and she didn't think Mandy was, either. And how would they ever split one computer between them? And of course there was Elizabeth. She deserved some credit, too.

"That's right!" Mrs. Arnette continued delightedly. "A computer for the whole school to use! And Elizabeth and Amy have won a big new dictionary for the library."

"Oh," Jessica said, feeling very disappointed. "I see. The prizes are for the school."

"Isn't that wonderful?" Mrs. Arnette said. "Just think how proud you'll be when you see all your classmates using the computer *you* helped bring to Sweet Valley Middle School."

Jessica sighed. "I'm sure I'll be very proud," she said. It would have been wonderful if the prize had been a trip to Disneyland or tickets to a Dynamo concert, she thought. Still, it would be terrific to perform in front of a live audience at the festival. And she knew that even if Mandy couldn't be in the act, she'd be very pleased to know they had won. Jessica couldn't wait to tell her.

On the way to Mandy's house Jessica stopped at the florist and bought a little bouquet of daisies. When she finally got to the Millers', it was almost four o'clock.

Cecilia answered the doorbell. "Hello, Jessica," she said, smiling. "Mandy will be so glad to see you. She's upstairs with the others."

"The others?" Jessica asked.

Cecilia nodded happily and glanced down at Jessica's bouquet. "It's so nice of all of you to come see her and bring so many beautiful flowers. I know Mandy is absolutely thrilled to see how many friends she has."

To her dismay, Jessica discovered that Mandy's room was filled with Unicorns. The Unicorns were just as surprised to see Jessica, and every bit as uncomfortable.

"Er, ah, hello, Jessica," Janet said uneasily. "We, uh, er, didn't expect to see you here."

"I, ah, didn't expect to see you, either," Jessica said. She glanced around the room. They were all there, Lila, Janet, Mary, and all the rest. There were so many Unicorns piled on the bed that Jessica couldn't even see Mandy.

"I think I'll come back another time," Jessica

said as she edged toward the door. She had looked forward to being with Mandy. But with all these people hanging around, she'd never get a chance to talk with her. She couldn't help but feel jealous and resentful, too. Mandy was *her* special friend, and the Unicorns supposedly didn't even like her.

Janet looked relieved that Jessica was leaving. "Well, if you think you *have* to go . . ." she said, and let her voice trail off.

But then Jessica heard Mandy calling from the bed.

"Is that Jessica who just came in?" she asked. "Don't go, Jessica!"

Kimberly Haver moved aside and Jessica could see Mandy, propped up against the pillows. She looked much better than she had the last time Jessica had seen her. She looked as if she were almost back to her old self, smiling and cheerful. And much to Jessica's surprise, she looked as if she were having a terrific time being the center of the Unicorns' attention.

"Uh, Jessica," Janet said, "I think I'd better explain."

"Explain what?" Jessica asked.

"The reason we didn't invite you to come with us this afternoon," Janet said in a low voice as she pulled Jessica to where Mandy couldn't hear them. "The truth is, we didn't think you'd want to see Mandy. And we knew she wouldn't want to see you."

"Not want to see her?" Jessica exclaimed. "But she's my—"

"Well," Janet said, ignoring Jessica's protest, "you were the one who told Mandy she couldn't be a Unicorn. Everybody figured she was pretty mad at you. That's why it didn't seem . . . well, very tactful to invite you. And that's why we didn't ask you to chip in on the flowers, either, or to sign the get-well card."

Now Jessica had the answers to her questions. But instead of being relieved, she felt her temper flare. What right did the Unicorns have to assume Mandy didn't like her, or that she didn't like Mandy? But then Jessica remembered the Unicorns didn't know she and Mandy were real friends. She'd carefully kept their friendship a secret in order to avoid having the Unicorns give her a hard time. Her anger suddenly evaporated.

"Well," she said, "it looks as if everybody's having a good time, including Mandy." The Unicorns were laughing at a comic story Mandy had just told about her stay in the hospital. Lila posed with her arm around Mandy while Betsy took a picture.

Janet nodded. "I wonder," she mused, as if she were thinking out loud, "whether we've misjudged Mandy."

"Misjudged her?" Jessica asked. "What do you mean?"

Janet gave a start. "Oh, nothing," she said. Then she clapped her hands to get everybody's attention. "We'd better be going," she announced. "We don't want to tire Mandy."

Five minutes later, everybody but Jessica had left the room. Jessica sat on Mandy's bed.

"Whew," Mandy said. "What a mob!"

"I was surprised to find them here," Jessica said, handing Mandy the bunch of daisies she had brought.

"I was surprised, too," Mandy said. She accepted Jessica's flowers gratefully. "But I have to admit, I loved every minute of their visit." She handed Jessica a fancy box. "Especially Ellen's chocolates! Where did she get them, anyway?" Mandy imitated Lila's arch, sophisticated tone. "They're so delicious, they're positively *sinful.*"

Jessica smiled and took a bite of an expensive chocolate. "You look great," she said, looking critically at her friend.

"I feel good, too," Mandy said earnestly. "Except I get tired pretty easily and my scar itches." She leaned back against the pillows. "But I feel absolutely *terrific* when I remember that pretty soon I'm going to be normal again."

Jessica grinned. "You'll feel even better when I tell you about the act."

"The act?" Mandy asked. "You mean, the one the Hairnet entered in the 1920s festival?"

"That's the one," Jessica said nonchalantly. "The act that won first place."

Mandy's eyes opened wide. "First place! *Fabulous!*"

"Yes, and that's not all," Jessica continued. "Elizabeth and Amy's entry won second prize."

"Second prize? That's great!"

"And there's more," Jessica said.

"What more could there be?" Mandy asked.

Jessica laughed. "They want us to perform our act at the festival a week from tomorrow—in Hollywood!"

"Hollywood?" Mandy cried. "Didn't I tell you we'd get to Hollywood?" Then she groaned. "But my doctor will never let me go to Hollywood and bounce around on the stage a week from tomorrow. You and Elizabeth will have to do the act together." She brightened. "But he might let me be part of the audience if I promise not to do anything demanding, like clap or whistle."

"Do you think he would? That would be perfect!" Jessica exclaimed. "And one more thing," she added, adopting her most dramatic voice. "The prize for this terrific first-place act is—" She paused for effect.

"Well?" Mandy leaned forward. "Come on,

Jessica," she urged, "don't give me a hard time. What's the prize?"

"A computer."

"A computer?" Mandy asked incredulously. "How are we supposed to split one computer between two people? Three, counting Elizabeth. She deserves to get part of the prize, too."

"That's what I wanted to know," Jessica said. "Then the Hairnet set me straight. The computer is for the school, not for us." She pulled herself up and mimicked Mrs. Arnette's voice. " 'Just think how proud you'll be when you see all your classmates using the computer *you* helped bring to Sweet Valley Middle School!' Elizabeth and Amy have won a dictionary for the library."

Mandy burst into gales of laughter. When she finally stopped, she said, "I don't know what I'd do without you, Jessica. You are without doubt one of the greatest comediennes of all time! You always make me laugh." Then she grew a little serious. "I've got something else to thank you for, too. You remember that afternoon we got into the fight over the feather boa?"

Jessica nodded. "I've been feeling a little guilty about that," she confessed.

"Well, don't," Mandy said firmly. "If I hadn't fallen over that trunk and bumped my ribs, I might not have noticed the lump. And that's when I finally decided to go to the doctor, you know. The lump, and the flu I couldn't get rid of, made me so miserable I just had to do something. If it hadn't been for you and the feather boa, I might not have found out I had cancer until— well, until it was too late." She grinned. "So in honor of that unforgettable moment, I give you— *this!*"

Mandy reached behind her pillow and with a flourish pulled out the two pieces of the feather boa. "I'll keep half and you can keep half," she said. "To remind us of how lucky we were to get into such a terrific fight!"

Nine

◆

For the next week, everything went smoothly. Mandy wasn't back in school yet, but she was doing well. Jessica had almost completely forgotten how upset she had been with the Unicorns, and the Unicorns seemed to have forgotten they'd once tried to get rid of Mandy. They still sent her little presents and get-well notes. Occasionally, Jessica still thought they were paying attention to Mandy to make themselves look good. But more and more Jessica suspected that they had actually grown to like her.

On the Saturday of the silent-film festival, Mrs. Wakefield drove Jessica, Elizabeth, Amy, Mandy, and Mrs. Miller to the museum in Hollywood. While the twins were backstage putting on their costumes, Jessica peeked out through the stage curtains for a glimpse of Mandy and Amy. To her surprise, she saw somebody else she knew. It was Mrs. Arnette. There were quite a few other people in the audience, too, waiting for their act and for the museum's special film program.

But the biggest surprise of all came when the twins went on stage to perform. A TV-news crew had arrived to film their act! Jessica was momentarily struck with stage fright, but she quickly recovered and the girls turned in a terrific performance. When it was over, the audience applauded loudly. Mrs. Arnette clapped harder than anyone.

Finally the MC came out on the stage to award them a certificate the school could trade for a computer.

"Somebody else should be up here with us," Jessica said into the mike as the MC handed her the certificate. "Her name is Mandy Miller. She wrote most of the material for the act and starred in the original performance. She couldn't perform today because she's recovering from an operation. But she's in the audience. Could she come up to the stage?"

The MC smiled. "Will Mandy Miller join us?" he asked. The audience applauded as Mandy slowly climbed the steps to the stage and took her place beside Jessica and Elizabeth. Jessica felt very happy as she stood between Elizabeth and Mandy while the TV cameras filmed their triumph. Later, Amy came up on the stage, and she and Elizabeth accepted their prize for second place.

There were more surprises to come. The local Sweet Valley television station aired the story on the Sunday evening news. The station showed a brief clip of the twins' performance, and a shot of the three girls on stage.

Mandy saw the program, too, and called Jessica as soon as it was over. "Jessica, you and Elizabeth looked *terrific* on TV," she said. "No wonder our act won first place!" She giggled. "I'm glad they chose the unicorn joke."

Jessica wasn't sure the Unicorns would be glad the news had decided to air that particular joke. To her astonishment, though, she received a phone call from Janet later that evening.

"I just wanted to say how terrific you were on TV, Jessica," Janet said approvingly. "Your costumes were great, and I really had to laugh at the joke about the unicorn in purple sneakers. Did Mandy really make that up?"

Jessica was relieved that Janet wasn't angry about the joke. "Mandy made up most of the act," she said proudly.

"Um," Janet said thoughtfully. "I'll have to call Mandy and congratulate her, too, I guess."

The following week, Mandy came back to school part-time, often just to pick up her homework assignments. On the days when she had radiation treatments, Jessica dropped by her house after school to give her her work. Mandy was always happy to see her, even when she didn't feel well.

"I've got news for you, too, good news and bad news. The good news is that I get to go back to school full-time next week," Mandy said.

"Terrific!" Jessica hesitated. "What's the bad news?"

"The bad news is that it's happened!" Mandy cried tragically, yanking off the red wig and striking a dramatic pose. "Hair today, gone tomorrow."

Jessica stared at her friend. Overnight, most of her hair had fallen out. What was left was dull and lifeless.

"Oh, no!" Jessica exclaimed.

"I'm not vain," Mandy said, pulling a tuft of hair from her head and examining it. "But I loved my hair. I'd have given anything for this not to have happened." Mandy paused. "Well, maybe not *anything*," she conceded with a sad little laugh. "I mean, considering the alternative, I guess I'd rather lose my hair."

"But what are you going to do?" Jessica asked.

Mandy shrugged. "Get a wig, I guess," she said wryly. She picked up the red wig and looked at it. "Obviously I can't wear this one. I'd look like a dust mop. And I can't go around totally bald, either." She frowned. "The trouble is, wigs cost a lot of money. Mom says she'll try to get me one before I go back to school. In the meantime—" She reached behind her pillow and pulled out a baseball cap. The words "Brooklyn Dodgers" were printed on it in big letters. "It's a little out-of-date," she said, giggling. "It's the one we found in the trunk."

Jessica laughed at the way Mandy looked in the old baseball cap. "It's not bad," she said. "All you need is a catcher's mitt and Coach Cassels will sign you up for the season."

"Or, if you don't like baseball," Mandy said, "how about this?" She yanked off the cap and pulled on a crisp white captain's hat adorned with a brass insignia and the words "Coast Guard." She snapped a sharp salute. "Captain Miller reporting for duty, *sir!*"

Jessica giggled.

"But this is the very best one," Mandy said. She took off the captain's hat and replaced it with a blue velvet turban decorated with a huge rhinestone pin. "Meet Madame Amanda, ze greatest fortune-teller in ze universe." Mandy frowned. "Now, if ze madame could only remember where she left ze crystal ball—"

Jessica laughed until her sides ached. The

sight of blue-turbaned Madame Amanda was one of the funniest things she'd ever seen. She laughed even harder when Madame Amanda held up a water glass and proclaimed in a dramatic voice, "I look deep into ze future and I see . . . a *wig!*"

But deep inside, Jessica knew Mandy was laughing to cover up her sadness. She knew how upset Mandy must be over the loss of her beautiful hair. Only somebody very brave could clown around when she really felt terrible, and Jessica had to blink back tears when she thought of her friend's special kind of courage.

Two days later, on Friday afternoon, Jessica received a phone call from Mandy. At first, Mandy was giggling so hard Jessica could hardly understand her.

"You'll never believe what happened, Jess," Mandy said finally. "I've been crying about it for the past hour."

"But you're laughing now," Jessica pointed out.

"That's because the stupid thing is so ridiculous I had to stop crying and start laughing," Mandy answered sadly. She hiccuped loudly. "You know I'm supposed to go back to school on Monday."

"I know," Jessica said. "Everybody's looking

forward to it." In fact, their social-studies class was planning a surprise welcome-back party.

"I was looking forward to it, too," Mandy said, in a voice so comically mournful Jessica had to smile. "But not anymore. Something awful has happened, Jessica. It's so horribly, incredibly awful you can't even imagine it."

"What is it?" Jessica asked anxiously. "What's wrong, Mandy?"

"My mother has bought me a *wig!*" Mandy exclaimed.

"But I thought you wanted a wig," Jessica replied.

"Yes, but that was before I saw this one." Mandy hiccuped again. "Jessica," she added solemnly, "it has got to be the ugliest wig in the entire world."

"What does it look like?" Jessica asked.

Mandy paused and then asked, "Do you remember Little Orphan Annie?"

"Of course," Jessica replied. "My parents took me to see the musical when it came to San Francisco." Jessica's eyes widened. "Mandy, you don't mean—"

"This wig," Mandy said dramatically, "is an Annie wig."

"Oh, no!" Jessica exclaimed. "Mandy, that's not your style at all! Annie had curly red hair!"

"Yeah," Mandy said dejectedly. "I feel kind

of strange as a redhead. And what's worse, the wig is totally fake. I look exactly like a twelve-year-old baldie with a phony wig. And I have to wear this thing for eight or nine months, until my hair grows back."

Jessica didn't know what to say. How could Mandy come to school in a phony-looking Little Orphan Annie wig? Everybody would laugh at her. Then she sighed. Mandy's mother had probably bought the only wig she could afford. Jessica knew she should try to cheer Mandy up and help her to accept the fact that she had to wear it.

"Wait a minute, Mandy," she said. "Maybe we're looking at this from the wrong angle. Don't forget, Annie was a hit musical. The actress who played her became a big star. Who knows what it'll do for your career in show business?"

Mandy gave a short laugh. "Good try, Jessica. But it doesn't matter how you look at this wig— up, down, or sideways. It still looks ugly." She sighed. "But don't tell my mom that, OK? She's not crazy about the stupid wig either. In fact, she apologized when she gave it to me. It was the only one she could find in our price range."

"I wish I could do something to help," Jessica said.

"You already have," Mandy replied. "Maybe I *will* make a fortune with that hair, doing Annie impressions." She paused. "Would you mind if I hang up now? I think I'm going to lock myself in the bathroom and have another good cry."

After Jessica had hung up, she stared blankly at the phone. There had to be something she could do. She was still thinking when the phone rang again.

"Hi, Jessica," Lila said breathlessly. "Listen, Janet just phoned. She's called an emergency meeting of the Unicorns."

"Tonight?" Jessica asked in surprise.

"Yes, tonight," Lila said firmly. "She said it was extremely urgent. Everyone's got to attend. No excuses."

"But what's it about?"

"I don't know," Lila replied. "Janet wouldn't say. She just said it was important."

An hour later, the Unicorns were assembled in the Howells' huge recreation room. Janet stood in front of them.

"I know you're wondering why I asked you here tonight," she said. "It's about Mandy Miller."

"Mandy Miller?" Lila and Ellen exclaimed in unison. A ripple of conversation ran around the room.

"Mandy?" Jessica asked. "What about her?"

"I've been thinking," Janet continued, "that we might have made a mistake when we turned Mandy down. Maybe we should reconsider."

Jessica's mouth fell open. She couldn't believe what she was hearing. Janet Howell was actually proposing Mandy Miller as a new member!

There was more excited talk, and Janet raised her hand. "I know what you're thinking," she said when everybody had quieted down. "You're all thinking it was my idea to have Jessica get rid of Mandy. Mine and Lila's, that is."

"And Ellen's," Lila added hurriedly.

"Right," Janet said. "But in the past few weeks, since Mandy's been sick, all of us have had a chance to get to know her better. I think most of us would agree that she's . . . well, she's different from what we thought."

"She's still not exactly Unicorn material," Ellen put in. She looked a bit annoyed. "I'll bet when she comes back to school on Monday, she'll be wearing one of those weird outfits of hers—with her purple sneakers. I hear she's losing her hair from all that radiation, too. She'll probably be wearing a wig."

Jessica sighed. Ellen would never believe the kind of wig Mandy would be wearing on Monday.

"Maybe she isn't the kind of person we would normally think of as a Unicorn," Janet admitted. "But maybe it isn't so great that all the Unicorns are exactly alike. Maybe we need some variety. When Mandy's around, she puts things into a . . . well, a different light."

"I agree," Mary said. "When Mandy's around, I laugh a lot. She's got a way of making everything fun."

Janet turned to Jessica. "You were the one who gave Mandy the bad news, Jessica. What do you think she'll say when we tell her we've changed our minds?"

Jessica remembered how hurt Mandy had been. "I don't think Mandy will agree to join," she said. "She was pretty upset at us when we turned her down. In fact, she said she wouldn't be a Unicorn for a million dollars."

Janet frowned. "Maybe she'll change her mind. I think it's worth a try. Let's take a vote on it. We can do it by secret ballot."

When the ballot was taken, there were only two votes against Mandy. Jessica still couldn't believe it. Mandy Miller was really going to be invited to be a Unicorn! Of course, Mandy wouldn't accept. But she might be glad they asked her.

Jessica stood up. "Listen, everybody," she said. "Now that we've voted, I need to tell you about Mandy's big problem. No, make that her *wig* problem."

Several Unicorns giggled. "Jessica," Lila said sternly, "would you stop making jokes and get to the point?"

"What's the problem?" Mary asked.

"You've all heard that Mandy's losing her hair because of the radiation," Jessica said. "She'll have to wear a wig for several months until her hair grows back."

Everybody nodded. "It might be kind of fun to have a wig," Betsy Gordon said.

"Yes, if you could have your own hair, too," Kimberly Haver responded. "It would be awful to have to wear a wig because you're bald."

"Today, Mrs. Miller bought a wig for Mandy," Jessica went on. "It's the best wig the Millers can afford, but it's not exactly Mandy's style." She paused. "In fact, Mandy says it reminds her of Little Orphan Annie's hair."

"How do you know all this, Jessica?" Lila asked suspiciously.

Jessica looked straight at Lila. "Because Mandy told me," she said. "Mandy's a good friend. I've been seeing a lot of her even before she got sick." Jessica wondered how the others were going to react to her confession. But nobody seemed at all surprised or disturbed.

"A Little Orphan Annie wig!" Ellen shuddered. "How horrible."

"I can't imagine wearing something like that on my head," Kimberly said, stroking her own black hair.

"Poor Mandy," Mary said sympathetically. "Is there any way we can help?"

"Maybe," Jessica said. "We could buy her another wig."

"Wouldn't that be pretty expensive?" Belinda Layton asked doubtfully. "I've heard that a good wig costs a lot of money."

"Yes, it might cost a lot," Jessica admitted. "But I have an idea. Why don't we use the money we were going to spend on our party on a new wig for Mandy? It might even make her change her mind about us."

"Jessica!" Ellen exclaimed. She sounded horrified. "You can't be suggesting we cancel our party!"

Jessica thought of Mandy in her awful wig, and the thought gave her courage. "That's exactly what I'm saying," she replied firmly. "We can use our party money, plus any other money we can scrounge up." She looked straight at Ellen. "How would *you* like to go around for almost a year wearing a hideous wig?"

Ellen was silent.

Janet cleared her throat. "I think Jessica has a very interesting idea," Janet said. "We don't actually have to cancel the party, just postpone it for a little while." She smiled generously. "And I'll be glad to donate my allowance for this month."

Not to be outdone, Lila spoke up. "I'll donate

my allowance, too," she said, "and I'll ask my father for some extra money."

Ellen sighed. "Me, too," she said, and there was a chorus of agreement from the rest of the Unicorns.

"Terrific!" Jessica exclaimed. "Let's go wig shopping first thing in the morning. Maybe we can find one exactly like Mandy's real hair."

The Unicorns agreed to meet in the mall at ten o'clock the next morning, in front of Parker's Wig Salon. Each member promised to bring all the money she could get her hands on. As Jessica walked home that night, she couldn't help but smile. She had thought the Unicorns were self-centered and stuck-up. But now they were doing something very generous for somebody else. The Unicorns, she decided, really were friends she could be proud of.

Ten

◇

"This has got to be the weirdest thing I've ever done," Lila said as she took a long brown braid from a box full of hairpieces.

Jessica giggled. The Unicorns were gathered in Parker's Wig Salon, trying to select a wig for Mandy. The shelves of the small shop were crowded with plastic wig stands bearing wigs of all colors and styles. Some were long and layered, others were short and curly. Jessica spotted one that looked shaggy, like a sheepdog, and another that looked as if it might have been worn by the Wicked Witch in *The Wizard of Oz*.

Mary pulled on Jessica's sleeve. "Look at *that* one!" she said. It was a short, frizzled red wig, splotched with blue and spangled with glitter. "Who would wear a thing like that?"

A saleswoman came up to them. "That's the kind of wig we sell to circus clowns," she replied.

Janet stepped forward. "We're looking for a wig for a girl who's lost her hair because of radiation treatments. It has to be dark brown, like her natural hair color."

"And long, too," Jessica added. "Mandy's real hair hung down to her waist."

"I don't think your friend would want a long wig," the saleswoman said thoughtfully. "It would be very heavy and hard to keep in place when she's playing games or swimming. It would be hard to take care of, too."

Jessica sighed. It would be nice to get a wig exactly like Mandy's own hair, but she hadn't thought of the problems.

"You mean, she can wear her wig when she's swimming?" Kimberly asked curiously.

"As long as she uses special tape," the saleswoman replied. She smiled at them. "Your friend can wear the wig all the time, except when she's sleeping—or roasting marshmallows."

"Roasting marshmallows?" Jessica asked. "Why?"

"Heat from a fire frizzes most wigs," the saleswoman told them. "And she won't wear it at night because the wig would get rumpled." She turned to a shelf and took down a light brown curly wig. "What do you think about this one?"

Lila frowned doubtfully. "Mandy's real hair is darker."

"And it isn't very curly," Mary said.

Jessica noticed another wig. The hair was straight, and it was almost the shade of Mandy's hair. It had a kind of pixieish look Mandy might like. "How about that one?" she asked. She glanced at the price tag. It was expensive, seventy dollars, but with all the money the Unicorns had scraped together, they could afford it.

"It's cute," Kimberly said approvingly.

Janet nodded. "I like it," she said. "Why don't you model it for us, Jessica?"

"It's not exactly my color," Jessica said, "but OK."

The saleswoman took the wig off its stand and Jessica sat down in a chair in front of a mirror. Quickly, the saleswoman pinned up Jessica's hair and then pulled on the wig. Jessica stared at herself in the mirror. She'd always wondered what she would look like with dark hair. Now she knew.

"Is that *you*, Jessica?" Lila asked with a giggle.

"How do I look?" Jessica asked, posing like a model.

"Like a pixie," Mary said.

"Really cute," Ellen agreed.

"If you want to surprise your friend, you could take the wig now," the saleswoman suggested. "She could bring it back later to have it fitted."

"We'll take it," Janet decided. "It's perfect for Mandy. It's exactly the way her hair would have looked if she'd gotten it cut."

Jessica was delighted. But at the same time she was worried. Would Mrs. Miller be upset that they had bought Mandy another wig to replace the one she had bought?

Five minutes later the Unicorns were on their way to Mandy's house, carefully carrying the wig box. The box contained not only Mandy's new wig, but a wig stand, a wig brush, and special wig shampoo, all gifts from the Unicorns.

When they knocked at the Millers' door, Archie answered. He had a peanut-butter-and-banana sandwich in one hand, and Iggy was perched on his shoulder.

Ellen shrieked and backed away. "It's a lizard!"

"It's only an iguana," Jessica said calmly. "He won't bite." She smiled at Archie. "Is Mandy home?"

He nodded and took a bite of his sandwich. "She's in the basement," he said, "looking in the trunk for hats to wear over her wig."

Jessica laughed. "Can we go down?" she asked.

"Sure," Archie said. He turned to Ellen. "Want to hold Iggy?" he asked. There was a wicked glint in his eye as he reached for his iguana.

"No!" Ellen cried, and scurried behind Jessica.

"Come on," Jessica said, and led them all down to the basement.

Mandy looked up in surprise when she saw the Unicorns crowd into the room. Her Annie wig was lying on the floor, and on her head she wore a striped railroad engineer's cap and a red bandanna. "Hi!" she grinned. "All aboard!"

Everybody laughed. Even without her hair, Mandy was cute. Her cheeks were pink and healthy-looking, and she wasn't so thin anymore.

"You're really looking great, Mandy," Lila complimented her. She was hiding the wig box behind her back. "You're gaining weight."

Mandy grinned ruefully. "Yeah, I look just like any other bald girl my age." She laughed. "Want to see my new wig?" When everybody nodded, she tossed off the engineer's cap and tugged on the wig.

The girls were silent. The wig was so awful, nobody knew exactly what to say.

Mandy grinned and flicked one of the bright

red ringlets. "It is truly outrageous, isn't it? All I need is a red dress and a pair of tap shoes, and I'm ready for Hollywood." She did a little tap dance.

Janet took the wig box from Lila and handed it to Jessica. "Here, Jessica," she whispered, "you give it to her."

"Uh, Mandy," Jessica said hesitantly, "we've got something for you."

"What is it?" Mandy asked. Her eyes widened when she saw the wig box. They widened still more when she opened the box and saw what was inside.

"It's a wig!" she cried. "Is it for me?" she asked. Then she laughed delightedly. "Of course it's for me! You guys all have your own hair."

"Go on," Ellen urged. "Try it on."

"Yes," Lila said. "Try it on, Mandy. We want to see how you look."

A moment later, a new Mandy stood in front of the Unicorns. "I can't believe it," she breathed as she looked at herself in the little mirror Lila had pulled out of her purse. "You guys bought this for *me*? It must have cost a fortune!"

"We postponed our party," Janet said. Jessica could tell she enjoyed being generous.

"And pooled our allowances," Belinda added.

"And some of our parents chipped in," Lila said proudly.

"I hope you don't mind that the wig is short," Jessica added. "The lady at the wig shop said a long-haired wig would be heavy and hard to take care of. You can bring this one back to get it fitted."

"I like it," Mandy said, still gazing at herself in the mirror. "No, I *love* it! It's truly the most wonderful hair anybody ever had." She blinked hard and looked around at the Unicorns. "Wow, thanks, you guys."

"Hello, girls," Mrs. Miller called from the top of the stairs. "There are cookies and lemonade in the kitchen if you—" As Mrs. Miller caught sight of Mandy, she stopped.

"Do you like it, Mom?" Mandy asked. "The Unicorns gave it to me!"

"It's wonderful!" Mrs. Miller exclaimed. "It's so much nicer than the other one." She smiled at the Unicorns. "Mandy and I *both* thank you," she said.

When Mrs. Miller had gone back to the kitchen, Jessica turned to Mandy. "I'm relieved. I was worried your mom might be mad at us."

Janet cleared her throat. "We have something to tell you, Mandy," she said. She looked just a little uncomfortable. "When we turned you down for membership in the Unicorns, it was really because we didn't think we knew you well enough." She cleared her throat again and continued. "But now things are different. We've had a chance to get to know you. And we've changed our minds. We'd like you to be a Unicorn." Janet folded her arms and looked at Mandy expectantly.

Jessica watched Mandy closely. Janet's excuse for rejecting Mandy as a Unicorn had sounded pretty lame to her, and Janet's tone had been too confident. If Jessica thought Janet sounded arrogant, what must Mandy think? No matter how grateful Mandy was about the wig, she would still turn them down.

But to Jessica's surprise, Mandy seemed to be considering Janet's offer. She looked from one Unicorn to another. Then she said, "I'd like some time to think it over."

Janet looked disappointed, but she nodded. "I understand," she said. "Becoming a Unicorn is an important step. It isn't something you jump into."

Mandy grinned impishly. "Why don't we jump into some cookies and lemonade?"

As she followed the Unicorns upstairs, Jessica thought she knew why Mandy hadn't refused Janet's offer right away. Mandy probably wanted time to think of the most clever way to reject them.

Jessica stayed on after the other Unicorns had gone home. As the two girls washed the glasses, Jessica sneaked looks at her friend. She wished

Mandy would say something about the Unicorns' invitation.

Finally, she couldn't control her curiosity any longer. "OK," she said, flinging the dish towel onto the table. "If you're not going to tell me, I'll have to ask. What sort of scheme are you planning?"

Mandy looked puzzled. "Scheme?"

"For the Unicorns, I mean," Jessica said. She chose her words carefully. "You know how the Unicorns are. I wouldn't blame you a bit for thinking they're only interested in you because . . ."

"Because I have cancer?" Mandy asked bluntly. "Because all of a sudden, I've got a weird kind of popularity, sort of like Dracula?"

Jessica smiled. Only Mandy would see the humor in the situation. "I honestly think it's different with them this time," Jessica said. "I think Janet asked you because she and the other Unicorns genuinely like you. But when Janet gave her speech, it came out sounding . . . well, pretty arrogant. So I figured you asked for more time in order to come up with a good way to turn them down."

Mandy rinsed the last glass and turned off the faucet. When she spoke, her voice was serious. "Before, when I first wanted to be a Unicorn," she said, "it was because you guys were so popular and pretty. I thought that if I were a Unicorn,

I'd be popular, too." Mandy grinned. "Maybe I wouldn't become beautiful overnight, and I wouldn't suddenly be able to afford fancy clothes. But kids would overlook those things because I was a Unicorn."

"Mandy, I—" Jessica wanted to tell Mandy she *was* pretty, and that people *did* like her.

But Mandy held up her hand. "But when I got sick, I learned a lot about what matters and what doesn't. Being pretty and having fancy clothes *don't* matter. Having hair doesn't matter a lot, either." She grinned and reached up to touch her new wig. "But being *alive* does matter, and so does having friends who *care* about your hair." Her grin grew wider. "You guys are still the coolest girls in school. And my best friend's a Unicorn. So is it OK with you if I say yes?"

Jessica flung her arms around Mandy. "It's terrific with me!" she exclaimed. "Oh, Mandy, we're going to have such a great time together!"

"You bet," Mandy agreed. "And just wait until next year!"

"Next year?" Jessica asked.

"That's when I run for president of the Unicorns, of course," Mandy answered with a laugh.

On Monday Mandy returned to school, wearing her new wig. The first thing she did was find Janet and tell her she had decided to join the Unicorns. The next thing she did was find Caroline Pearce and tell her the news, too.

"That way," Mandy told Jessica as they headed to social-studies class, "everybody will know in a matter of minutes that I'm the newest Unicorn."

Jessica laughed. "Well, I'm just glad becoming a Unicorn hasn't changed your style." Mandy was wearing a pair of khaki-colored pants, a red T-shirt that said "Ski Bear Valley," her favorite old army fatigue jacket, and her purple sneakers. "Was Janet surprised when she saw your outfit?"

"Maybe a little surprised," Mandy said with a toss of her head. "But she'll get used to me."

But a moment later Mandy was the one who was surprised when she walked into social-studies class. A big banner spelled out "Welcome Back Mandy!" in huge letters. And she was even more surprised when Lila and Ellen began to pass out the refreshments they had brought for the class to enjoy.

But the biggest surprise of all came when Mandy saw that everybody in the class was wearing purple sneakers!

"Everybody looks as though they waded through a puddle of grape Kool-Aid," she said happily.

"I know," Jessica agreed. "Isn't it great?"

"And all this food! My little brother should

be here," Mandy said as she accepted a cupcake from Lila.

"I'm glad he's not," Jessica said, biting into a cookie. "Brothers are the worst. I'll take a sister over a brother any day."

"Having a little sister would be nice, wouldn't it?" Elizabeth said as she joined their group.

Jessica nodded. "I'm tired of being the youngest in the family. I'd like to have someone look up to *me* for a change!"

Will Elizabeth and Jessica's wish come true? Find out in Sweet Valley Twins #49, THE TWINS' LITTLE SISTER.

SWEET VALLEY TWINS™

Buy them at your local bookstore or use this handy page for ordering:

Bantam Books, Dept. SVT3, 2451 S. Wolf Road, Des Plaines, IL 60018

Please send me the items I have checked above. I am enclosing $_____
(please add $2.50 to cover postage and handling). Send check or money
order, no cash or C.O.D.s please.

Mr/Ms _____

Address _____

City/State _____ Zip _____

Please allow four to six weeks for delivery.   SVT3-4/92
Prices and availability subject to change without notice.

SWEET VALLEY TWINS™

☐	15681-0	TEAMWORK #27	$2.75
☐	15688-8	APRIL FOOL! #28	$2.99
☐	15695-0	JESSICA AND THE BRAT ATTACK #29	$2.75
☐	15715-9	PRINCESS ELIZABETH #30	$2.99
☐	15727-2	JESSICA'S BAD IDEA #31	$2.75
☐	15747-7	JESSICA ON STAGE #32	$2.99
☐	15753-1	ELIZABETH'S NEW HERO #33	$2.99
☐	15766-3	JESSICA, THE ROCK STAR #34	$2.99
☐	15772-8	AMY'S PEN PAL #35	$2.95
☐	15778-7	MARY IS MISSING #36	$3.25
☐	15779-5	THE WAR BETWEEN THE TWINS #37	$2.99
☐	15789-2	LOIS STRIKES BACK #38	$2.99
☐	15798-1	JESSICA AND THE MONEY MIX-UP #39	$2.95
☐	15806-6	DANNY MEANS TROUBLE #40	$3.25
☐	15810-4	THE TWINS GET CAUGHT #41	$3.25
☐	15824-4	JESSICA'S SECRET #42	$2.99
☐	15835-X	ELIZABETH'S FIRST KISS #43	$2.99
☐	15837-6	AMY MOVES IN #44	$3.25
☐	15843-0	LUCY TAKES THE REINS #45	$3.25
☐	15849-X	MADEMOISELLE JESSICA #46	$2.95
☐	15869-4	JESSICA'S NEW LOOK #47	$2.95
☐	15880-5	MANDY MILLER FIGHTS BACK #48	$3.25
☐	15899-6	THE TWINS' LITTLE SISTER #49	$2.99
☐	15911-9	JESSICA AND THE SECRET STAR #50	$3.25

Bantam Books, Dept. SVT5, 2451 S. Wolf Road, Des Plaines, IL 60018

Please send me the items I have checked above. I am enclosing $_____ (please add $2.50 to cover postage and handling). Send check or money order, no cash or C.O.D.s please.

Mr/Ms _____

Address _____

City/State _____ Zip _____

SVT5-11/92

Please allow four to six weeks for delivery.
Prices and availability subject to change without notice.